Autumn Deception

by

N. Jade Gray

Autumn Deception

Cover Art by *Tina Lynn Stout*

The Wild Rose Press, Inc.
PO Box 708
Adams Basin, NY 14410-0708
Visit us at www.thewildrosepress.com

Publishing History
First Edition, 2023
Trade Paperback ISBN 978-1-5092-5243-5
Digital ISBN 978-1-5092-5242-8

Published in the United States of America

He met her at the front of the car. "Do you need me to carry you?"

As tempting as his offer was, she cursed the fact he didn't need to bother. Tucking an errant curl behind her ear, she shook her head. "No. Clara has stepping-stones from the drive to the front steps. I should be fine." A board creaked under her weight as she treaded onto the porch. She peered into a window nearby. Through a crack in the curtain, she spied Gram.

The serene picture made her want to laugh hysterically. She sat in a rocker with her fingers flying with her crochet hook in her hands making her famous miniature red hearts. Beside her on the end table were a stack of finished ones. The tranquil scene caused her to shake her head. The big faker. She wouldn't be surprised if she was humming one of her favorite hymns while she worked.

"Is something wrong?"

The deep voice from behind jolted her back to the fact she wasn't alone. She stuttered a moment. "Just look…" Her hands fluttered. "Sitting there all innocent." She could feel an angry blush creeping over her body under the scratchy blanket. "Do you have your handcuffs on you?" In the dim light cast through the curtains a quizzical expression appeared on his face.

"Yes, ma'am."

"Well, keep them handy." She unclenched her fists by her sides. "I may strangle her!"

Praise

N. Jade Gray is the author of *All for the Love of a Cowboy*, *Raider of Her Heart*, *Tangled in Tinsel*, and *Kisses and Lemon Snowflake Cookies*.

Raider of Her Heart was a Finalist in 2019 with the Oklahoma Romance Writers of America International Digital Awards, was nominated in 2019 with the Paranormal Romance Guild for a Reviewers Choice Award, won a recommended read Reader Ready Award in 2020 from Author Shout, and was a Finalist in 2020 for a Raven Award with Uncaged Book Reviews.

Tangled in Tinsel won a recommended read Reader Ready Award in 2021 from Author Shout, voted Book of the Month by Long and Short Reviews (LASR) in 2021, and was a third place winner in the 2021 Book of the Year by Long and Short Reviews (LASR).

Dedication

To Mom and Dad
In honor of my mom, the red crocheted hearts
mentioned in Autumn Deception are called Joy's
Blessings. Mom crochets the hearts and hands them out
to bless and show love to the people she meets.

In loving memory of my dad, George, Autumn
Deception references Dooley's pond (grove), a pig
named Georgette, and a skunk in his honor. I just didn't
include the duck with the skunk. Because we've all
heard dad's story about where's the duck?

Thanks again to my editor, Nicole, for her guidance,
patience, and prodding. We got there!

Chapter One

"Ahem."

Startled Sierra Scott jerked awake. Her head felt like a ten-ton paperweight resting on her numbed hands. The grit in her eyes dislodged as she blinked at the blurred items littering her desk. It took a few moments for everything to come into focus. Her muscles in her back protested as she uncrossed her arms to sit upright. What had interrupted her sleep? Her gaze swung to her office doorway to snag on her grandmother, Cora Scott, and chief financial officer Mark Simons standing inside the opening.

"See, Mark. Like I said." Cora splayed her hands. "The poor girl could use a break."

Her grandmother's face radiated concern as Sierra grimaced and rose from her chair. "Mark." She glanced down and moved a takeout container from a Chinese restaurant aside to look at her appointment calendar. "Gram? Did we have a meeting?" The other two occupants in the room exchanged a glance with each other.

"No. Sierra."

The frown on Mark's face produced a wave of panic. Oh no. "Is something wrong with the building plans?" Gram crossed the floor and reached to remove something from her tangled hair. Had she fallen asleep on a lo mein noodle? Heat traveled to her cheeks at the wrinkled Post-it note Cora held out. At least it wasn't food. A grimace traveled up her spine as she accepted the discarded piece of paper.

"The exact opposite." Mark took a couple of steps farther into the room. "Cora is requesting I finish up the final meetings and paperwork while you take a well-deserved vacation."

The sleep fog had begun to dissipate over the last couple of minutes. *But this is my company. This was her responsibility.* Her gaze rested once again upon her grandmother. Even though the company transferred to her once her grandfather passed, Cora was reaffirming that she still wielded power. "Gram. I need to see this expansion through."

She placed an arm around her waist. "I know you do." She smoothed her hair back like she used to when she was a child. "But look at you. The dark smudges under your eyes. Post-it notes stuck in your hair and indentions from the pen you slept on when you rested, just for a moment I'm sure, on your desk. Gramps didn't intend for you to work yourself into an early grave. I'm worried about you."

"I knew what responsibilities I was taking on when I took over granddad's company." She eased away from her and splayed a hand encompassing the office. "Look at what I've accomplished since I've taken over."

Mark cleared his throat. "Sierra, you've done a wonderful job, but that's not the issue. Let your upper management earn their keep while you take time off. We have your cell number and Cora has left an address where you will be staying. Let us help."

"Where I'll be?" She raised an eyebrow in question. "And where will I be?" Gram beamed at her as if her inquiry hadn't been voiced in a sarcastic tone.

"Do you remember my friend Clara?"

The image of a petite older woman popped into her mind. "Vaguely. She attended Gramps funeral."

Her silver curls bobbed as she nodded. "She's invited us to Harts Valley for the apple festival. We can stay at her home. There is plenty of room."

Sierra placed a hand behind her neck and firmly massaged, trying to release the tension gaining ground there. "Sounds like you've thought of everything." The knots eased as she continued to knead her neck. "Except one tiny detail."

Cora frowned and asked, "What is that, dear?"

"My appointment calendar is booked solid." Apprehension stirred in her stomach. "I have more than the expansion vying for my time."

A smile spread across her face before she turned and left the office to come back in with her assistant, Janet, trailing behind her. "Janet. Tell my granddaughter she doesn't need to worry about her schedule."

The feeling of being railroaded joined the anxiety churning in her stomach. "Care to elaborate, Gram? I have so much on my plate at the moment."

"Don't worry, Sierra." Her assistant glanced from her to Cora. "We've hashed out everything. Your next two weeks are clear."

Of course it was. Her arguments were fast losing ground. "But the fall benefit?"

"Is handled. Anything needing your attention, I will send by courier."

She turned and crossed over to stare out her office window. The morning sun warmed her chilled arms. Not bothering to turn she addressed her guests, "You would think as an owner of a multi-million-dollar company I would have more control over a meddling grandmother."

"Sierra."

Her gaze swung to meet Mark's firm stare. "We care about you and your health. Don't think of this as punishment." He pivoted toward the door. "Now that the crisis was averted, I have work that needs my attention."

The office door silently clicked behind him as he retreated. When had she taken a vacation last? Was it sad she couldn't remember? Janet and Gram still stood with determination stamped across their foreheads. Their arms crossed as if ready for battle. Exhaustion pure and simple flowed through her body. They were right. If she didn't take a break, she was headed for an early grave at the tender age of thirty-two. "Gram?"

"Yes, dear?"

"Are you driving?" A sigh escaped. "Or am I?"

"You'll go?" A huge smile broke upon her face. "I'll let Clara know you're coming. Why don't you take your Jeep? Drive with the top off or windows down? Enjoy the cooler weather. I'll text you her address and meet you there."

Her grandmother exited as quickly as she had arrived. She turned toward her desk to collect her laptop. "If you will excuse me, Janet. It seems I need to go home and pack."

"Sierra?"

Her gaze met her assistant's. "Yes?"

"Enjoy. Rest easy and relish your time off."

****

"Come on, Sierra. Quit being such a wimp!"

A gasp tore from her throat as Gram, naked as a jaybird, cannon balled into the awaiting pond. The maneuver was well executed, as if she'd had lots of practice. Gone was the prim older woman who had visited her office hours before. She shook her head. "Gram, are you crazy?" She glanced about. "What if someone should see you?"

"Who cares." She gave a dismissive wave of her hand. "Let them look. It's been some time since I've gotten a good thrill."

A hysterical giggle hovered in her chest, waiting to make an exit. An unladylike snort echoed throughout the pasture instead. She placed a hand over her mouth and peeped about. "What about Clara?"

"What about her?" She executed a turn with her arms flowing above her head, as smooth as any ballet dancer.

"Isn't she expecting us back soon?" Her whispered question carried on the Oklahoma evening breeze.

"Not really. Besides, Clara can be such a fuddy-duddy. She didn't enjoy exposing her bosom the last time we swam."

The last time? Really? How often did she indulge in the activity? She stared at her backstroking grandmother in amazement. The exhaustion and burnout she'd felt this morning was replaced with shock.

A wave of water splashed her as a girlish giggle escaped her companion's lips. "I didn't realize a granddaughter of mine would be such a killjoy. Come on, slug bug. Shuck those clothes. I'm not getting any younger here."

Her lips firmed. "I'm no prude." She stomped away and tucked behind the nearest tree. Gram's laughter resonated in the waning light from the setting sun.

A rustle of grass made her jump. She paused in

unbuttoning her shirt. Two curious bovines stood at attention a few feet away, their stares intent. After a few moments, their mouths began working in unison as they chewed on their cuds. Had she ever stripped in front of such an attentive audience?

"Shoo. Nothing to see here." She fluttered her hands. "Go on." With a flip of their tails, they turned and lumbered off. She lifted her gaze to study the sunset hues gracing the sky. Several shades of orange blended together before tapering into a light purple reaching into the heavens. *This display of wonder couldn't be found within the four walls of an office.* With a shake of her head, she stiffened her resolve and finished undressing.

Peeking from around the tree, she perused the area. It was now or never. She made a mad dash to the edge of the pond and with awkward grace leapt into the water. A scream escaped and rent the air as she surfaced.

"A bit titillating, isn't it?" Her wicked chuckle bounced off the surrounding trees from a short distance away.

Her teeth clanked together furiously. The water was cooler than expected for mid-September. "You could have warned me."

"It's more fun for you to experience it firsthand. Would you have joined me if I told you the water was a bit frigid?"

"No." She cast a glare in her direction as she began to churn her legs. The movement soon acclimated her to the water and the chattering of her teeth eased. The last rays of the sun danced in dim determination upon the water before disappearing in a final hooray.

A smile tugged at her lips as she slid to her back. The tension in her shoulders eased as she leisurely glided back and forth. Maybe Gram was right. She'd needed this break. More than she realized. All worries over the expansion and the upcoming fall benefit drifted away.

"I think I'm getting wrinkles on my wrinkles." Gram's words carried on the slight breeze and jerked Sierra from her reverie. "I'm going to head back up to Clara's. Feel free to stay a little longer. No need to leave because I'm calling it an evening."

She opened her eyes and gazed above at the stars as they twinkled in the sky. Did the star above wink at her? The fanciful thought played in her mind a moment before she shook it away to recap the day in her head. This morning she'd woke sprawled across her desk. Her fingers trailed in the water by her sides. A chuckle shimmied out. The millionaire heiress of Scott Enterprises was buck-naked in a country pond. The photographers who hounded her every step would have a field day with this type of story.

An owl hooted. The forlorn noise caused a shiver to glide across her skin. How long had Gram been gone? She stood and started treading water. As mud oozed through her toes another laugh escaped.

Her merriment froze in her throat as a siren blared in the distance. She almost slipped on the muddy bank as she spied red and blue lights fast approaching. Had something happened to her grandmother on her way back to Clara's? A quiver of fear raced up her spine.

Beating a hasty exit from the pond, she picked her way across the hard ground. A curse escaped her lips as she stepped on something sharp. A cry of pain escaped as she stumbled. She hobbled to the nearby tree and squinted. She'd definitely lost track of time. Darkness had settled in along with a chill in the night breeze.

Goosebumps skittered across her skin as she searched for her pile of clothes. Where were they?

Panic careened through her body as she scanned the area. Did she have the wrong tree? A short distance away she spied a lone white sock. Had Gram taken her clothes by mistake?

The siren was suddenly silenced as the sound of tires crunching on gravel drifted to her ears. She peeked from her hiding place. The patrol car stopped adjacent to the pond and a figure emerged from the vehicle. Her heart raced as the silhouette of a drawn gun reflected in the beam of the car's headlights. Scooting farther behind the tree, she tried to make herself as small as possible. Her heart skipped a beat as her breathing escalated.

The policeman's voice reverberated in the stillness. "Is anyone out here?"

She gasped as a flashlight popped on and she could hear the shuffling of feet in the grass. What was she going to do? "I'm behind the tree. Please don't come any closer." She cringed at how squeaky her voice sounded in the night's stillness.

"I'm Sheriff Collins, ma'am. Are you okay?"

As the shaft of light swung in her direction, she cringed. "All is fine."

"We received a call about a disturbance. Are you sure everything's all right?"

Her brows dipped as she frowned. He must be referring to her earlier scream when she jumped in the water. "I assure you, I'm okay. I was getting ready to head back up the hill to where I'm staying." She cringed and shifted farther behind the tree as the beam of the flashlight swung in her direction. "Seriously, no worries!" Her gaze snagged on the lone sock a short distance away. The sliver of the moon above shone like a spotlight on the item, mocking her. Would the sheriff leave? She held her breath.

"It's dark and getting late. I'll escort you."

Could he feel the eye roll she executed? Peachy, just peachy. She cleared her throat. "I'm sure you have more urgent matters to attend to. You can go back to fighting crime." A shuffling noise reached her ears. Was he walking toward her? "Stop! Oh God, please stop. I can find my way back without help."

The approaching footfalls ceased. "Ma'am, I wouldn't feel right leaving you out here in the dark if you are hurt. Or if something is wrong."

A groan bubbled from her lips. Great. Dudley Doo Right in the flesh. She was going to throttle Gram. The police officer began to lumber closer again. The flashlight beam was almost upon the sock. Too close. She screamed in near panic, "I'm naked. Please. Don't come any closer."

"Did someone hurt you?" A hardness she'd not heard in his tone before crept into his voice. "I can call an ambulance."

She rested her chin on her chest. A sigh tumbled from her lips. All of this drama because her grandmother had thought she was a prude. "Officer?" What was his name again?

"Sheriff Collins, ma'am."

She inhaled and released a calming breath. "I've not met with any harm."

"Let me help you. I'll wait until you are dressed and escort you home."

A few feet away the cows were back, and they'd brought friends. All stared at her as if watching an action flick. Out loud she answered, "I wish the situation was that easy."

"Pardon me?"

Her sigh carried on the night wind. "I said I wish I could put my clothes on. I think my grandmother took my clothes."

The sheriff paused a moment before exclaiming, "On purpose?"

"Yes. I believe so."

A deep male chuckle startled her. "Now I'm beginning to see your dilemma."

"So, you'll leave?" Hope blossomed in her chest. "Forget you were ever here?"

"Sorry, no can do."

Was his voice laced with regret? Or amusement? A shaft of light from the flashlight cut closer to where she hid. She gasped as it lit upon a few toes not hidden by the tree. "Hey. Cut it out!" Another deep chuckle rent the air. He seemed to be enjoying her situation a tad too much.

****

Cade Collins felt the tension slip from his shoulders. Now he understood what he was facing, he let himself relax. He holstered his gun. When the call had come in from Clara Lakewood, she'd been near hysterics. She'd reported a terrifying scream, like someone was getting murdered. She assured them at the station it wasn't a screech owl.

He'd been on his way home and the closest to the scene. He needed to call the station and cancel the call for backup. If he didn't, there would be another patrol car showing up soon.

He turned, crossed to his open door, and reached for

the radio.

"Hey. Sheriff. Are you still there?"

Her voice cracked. She wasn't as brave as she was letting on. He smiled as he eased away from his cruiser. "I'm here. I was calling off my backup." A chuckle escaped as a female gasp echoed across the space between them. "I didn't figure you'd want another male member of my team showing up."

A huff of indignation rang out. "You got that right. Thank you."

"I have a blanket in my trunk. I'm going to fetch it. Then we can get you home." He could swear her sigh of relief reverberated on the quiet night air.

"Best news I've heard since you've arrived."

He opened his trunk and rooted around until he found the folded wool blanket. He gave it a firm shake. A few feet from the tree, he was instructed to toss the cover. Not to come any closer. "Now, where would the fun be in that?" His teasing question had the woman sputtering like a wet hen.

"Throw me the damn blanket and turn around. Please."

The please was tossed on as an afterthought. He carefully pitched the cover and turned his back. "Killjoy."

"You know. There's the word that got me into this mess. Never take the gauntlet thrown down by a mischievous senior citizen."

"I'll keep that in mind the next time it happens to me." The shuffling noises from behind stopped.

"You can turn around."

Cade twisted about to find a tall woman emerging from behind the tree to step into the light cast by his headlights. She was pulling on the bottom of the material, which fell about mid-thigh.

Her grumbling carried to his ears. "You call this a blanket? More like a throw. Geez."

"It's better than the alternative." He shook his head and smiled. "Don't you think?"

She tucked her soggy hair behind an ear and glanced in his direction. "I'm sorry. I didn't mean to sound ungrateful."

"No need to apologize. I'm sure if our roles were reversed, I'd be doing a lot of complaining." She took a step and cringed. "Let me guess. The shoes are missing in action as well."

"I'm afraid so."

He closed the distance between them and scooped her up into his arms. A squeal broke free from her lips as she struggled to keep the blanket in place.

"Hey. A little notice next time."

A light fragrance wafted to his nose as his thoughts contemplated the possibility of a next time. It had been a long time since a woman graced his arms. All too soon he placed her feet back on the ground as he opened the passenger door on his cruiser. "Your chariot awaits."

Chapter Two

With one hand on the hem of the blanket, Sierra slid into the front seat. A sigh of relief escaped when she didn't dislodge her covering. The sheriff crossed in front of the car, passing through the light cast by the headlights. He was tall. But she'd already guessed that by the ease with which he'd picked up her five-foot ten frame.

When the dome light lit, she glanced at the man easing into the car. She caught a glimpse of twinkling brown eyes before the door shut and the overhead glow was extinguished. A woodsy scent reached her nose as he leaned in toward the ignition.

"I don't believe I caught your name." He paused in turning the key and glanced in her direction. "Who do I have the honor of driving home?"

She tilted her head and replayed their conversation in her mind. He was right. She'd never told him her name. "I guess we skipped that part. I'm Sierra Scott."

His warm hand engulfed her extended one. "Nice to meet you, Ms. Scott."

What was his name again? He'd told her at least twice, she recalled. "I'm sorry. I know you told me your name, but I was kind of preoccupied at the time."

A chuckle rumbled in his chest. "Perfectly understandable. No worries. I'm Sheriff Cade Collins. At your service."

Realizing she still held his hand, she released it. "Well, I bet you have a bunch of crazy tales you've experienced in the line of duty. And thanks to Gram, we added to your repertoire."

"Sierra." He started the car and backed out onto the road. "The stories could fill a book."

The brief drive up the hill was made in silence. When they pulled in front of the house, a porch light glowed awaiting her return. She squirmed in her seat as she remembered the embarrassing scene at the pond. The sheriff probably thought she and Gram were certifiable nuts.

The door handle was cool to her touch as she started to open the door. "Thank you, Sheriff. For the ride, the blanket…" She splayed a hand. "Well, let's face it, for the rescue. I do appreciate it."

He stalled her exit by placing a hand on her bare arm. "I'll see you safely inside."

His touch left a trail of heat in its wake. "I know I can't change your mind, so I'm not even going to waste my breath."

He withdrew his hand and she shivered at the loss of warmth. She shook her head, opened the door, and exited.

He met her at the front of the car. "Do you need me to carry you?"

As tempting as his offer was, she cursed the fact he didn't need to bother. Tucking an errant curl behind her ear, she shook her head. "No. Clara has stepping-stones from the drive to the front steps. I should be fine." A board creaked under her weight as she treaded onto the porch. She peered into a window nearby. Through a crack in the curtain, she spied Gram.

The serene picture made her want to laugh hysterically. She sat in a rocker with her fingers flying with her crochet hook in her hands making her famous miniature red hearts. Beside her on the end table were a stack of finished ones. The tranquil scene caused her to shake her head. The big faker. She wouldn't be surprised if she was humming one of her favorite hymns while she worked.

"Is something wrong?"

The deep voice from behind jolted her back to the fact she wasn't alone. She stuttered a moment. "Just look…" Her hands fluttered. "Sitting there all innocent." She could feel an angry blush creeping over her body under the scratchy blanket. "Do you have your handcuffs on you?" In the dim light cast through the curtains a quizzical expression appeared on his face.

"Yes, ma'am."

"Well, keep them handy." She unclenched her fists by her sides. "I may strangle her!"

His deep chuckle followed her as she released a huge sigh. Turning the knob, she entered the house. "Gram?"

"In here, Sierra honey. How was your swim?"

As if she didn't know. She entered the sitting room to the sound of Gram counting as she worked on her project.

"Hi. How…" Her grandmother broke off her greeting as she looked at the man following her into the room. A frown knitted her brow before she continued, "Well, good evening." She tilted her head. "Are you the sheriff? What brings you out to our neck of the woods?"

Before he could comment, Clara, Gram's friend, bounded into the room. "How's my favorite grand…"

She broke off abruptly and glanced at Gram before stuttering, "You're not Travis. We were expecting my grandson."

"Sorry to disappoint you, Ms. Lakewood." He removed his hat and dipped his head in greeting. "I'm Sheriff Cade Collins. We met briefly awhile back. Your grandson introduced us."

A blush stained the older woman's face. "Of course, Sheriff. I remember. I didn't mean to sound rude. How are you this evening?"

Realization snaked down her spine. She glanced first at Gram and then Clara. The expression on their faces would have been comical if she wasn't worried about standing in the front room practically naked in an old woolen blanket. The interfering grannies were trying their hand at match making.

With a hand to her lips, she struggled to hide a smile as she reveled in Gram and Clara's foiled plans. She turned to the sheriff and took a tentative step backward once she realized how close he stood. His features were no longer hidden in the night's shadows. She'd been too concerned earlier about her lack of clothing to examine her rescuer.

The dusk had hidden his rugged good looks. He now held his cowboy hat in his hands. Without the adornment upon his head, she noticed silver streaks at his temples woven in his brown hair. His nose had a slight bump as if broken at one time, but it was his arresting dark brown eyes that captured her attention. Eyes were her weakness, especially twinkling brown ones. His gaze broke away from hers to travel south to where her hand fingered the hem of the blanket tucked neatly above her breasts. "Let me go slip into…" a nervous laugh escaped. The usual line was something more comfortable. "Well, anything." The twinkle in his eyes deepened as his lips quirked in a crooked smile. She almost tripped as she backed from the room. "I'll be back in a jiffy."

Her bedroom door closed with a soft click. She shook her head as she replayed the evening's events over in her mind. What had Clara and Gram been thinking? She covered her face with her hands. She'd taken her clothes off and Gram absconded with them. Embarrassment flooded her whole being once again. What could the sheriff be thinking?

The mattress sank as she sat on the edge of the bed. Gram's agenda over the last couple of weeks was blatantly obvious. To set her up with anyone but Michael Dunham, the attorney helping with the company's legal matters. The moment Cora met Michael she'd made it plain she didn't trust him. Her words *slick car salesman and he's only after your money* still echoed in her mind. She frowned and nibbled her lip. Michael had joined the law firm representing Scott Enterprises about two months ago. He'd made his interest known as soon as they were introduced. As of yet she'd dodged his invitations, but she was running out of excuses. She couldn't pinpoint what made her leery about going out on a date, but there was something.

Muted laughter jarred her thoughts and she rose to dress. When she entered the sitting room, she paused. The only occupants were Gram and Clara.

Her grandmother eased up from the rocker. "The sheriff had to leave." She tucked her crochet into a bag by the chair. "His daughter wasn't feeling well."

"Oh." She fiddled with the wool clasped in her hands. It was hard to decide if the burst of disappointment was from him leaving without saying goodbye or if it was because he was married. She scolded herself. Why did she care if the rugged sheriff was married? "Well, then. I'll return the blanket when I'm in town." A crafty look passed between the two older women.

Clara shot a smile in her direction. "I'll be happy to give you directions to the police station. Maybe you'll run into my grandson, Travis, while you are there."

The blanket fell to the floor unforgotten as Sierra crossed her arms and stared at the geriatric duo.

"What?" Gram hitched her chin into the air.

The wheels in her brain began to churn. She'd been correct. This whole evening was a set up to meet Clara's grandson. She'd bet the lone sock deserted by the pond she was correct. She unlocked her arms and shook a finger at her grandmother. "Of all the stunts you've pulled in my thirty-two years of life, this had to be the most embarrassing. What were you two thinking?"

Clara fidgeted under her scrutiny a moment before she answered. "Travis is such a fine young man. We wanted to see if you'd hit it off."

"You got me naked. And stole my clothes." *One… Two… Three…* She took a calming breath as she silently counted. "Did it ever cross your minds to introduce us like normal people?" She studied their faces. "By the blank look upon your faces, I can see it didn't."

Gram came to her friend's defense. "Don't scold Clara. I fess up, it was my master plan."

She threw her hands into the air. "Shocker."

Her grandmother crossed the room and placed an arm around her shoulders. "Would you let us introduce Travis or any young man to you if we asked? I'm worried you're going to settle and start dating Michael."

The anger slipped away from her body. "Oh, Gram. I know you mean well, but don't you think I'm smart enough to make my own decisions?"

"There are days I'm not so sure."

The sparkle radiating from Gram's eyes made her laugh. She rested her head against her grandmother's forehead. "Please tell me there aren't any more plans to swim while we are on vacation."

Gram wiggled her brows. "How about fishing?"

She couldn't remember the last time she had time to cast a line. The activity normally would sound relaxing, but she'd need to be on her toes with Gram. "Where did you have in mind?"

"Down the hill at Dooley's grove."

She started to shake her head as her gaze followed Gram's pointing finger. There was no way she was going to return to the scene of the crime this soon, not even to retrieve the solo sock. "At the pond? Go ahead, Gram. I'll pass."

Chapter Three

Dust motes danced in the morning light through the open blinds as Cade shuffled paperwork on his desk. Where did he put the list for the extra security volunteers for the apple festival? He swore it was in the pile to the left. When the heap didn't yield what he searched for, he sighed and ran a hand through his hair.

A loud creak sounded from his chair as he leaned back and locked his fingers behind his head. His traitorous thoughts wandered to the previous evening. The image of Sierra Scott wearing nothing but the old scratchy wool blanket teased his mind. He'd not been given a real good glimpse of the total package until they'd stepped into the well-lit sitting room at Clara Lakewood's home. It was hard to tell what color her shoulder length hair was since it hung in a damp tangled mess, but her hazel eyes sparkled with humor. The shy smile she'd cast his way before leaving the room had teased his dreams all night.

He scoffed and placed his feet firmly on the floor. What was he doing? He was acting like a silly teenage boy who'd seen his first risqué photo. Not a forty-year-old single dad.

The pull of attraction he'd felt had come as a surprise. It had been years since he'd experienced the immediate pull he had last night. Not since the night he met Riley's mom, Melissa. He waited for the familiar pain associated with thoughts of his late wife but was somewhat startled when they didn't come.

He'd met Melissa at a college party, three doors down from the house he'd rented with his buddies. She was arriving with her friends as he was leaving. The bump into each other was a pure accident, but he'd felt an immediate connection. She'd looked at him from beneath her lashes and said excuse me with a shy smile gracing her lips.

He smiled at the memory. Instead of continuing out the door, he'd stayed and fallen in love.

"Sheriff."

The firm knock brought him out of his memories. With a glance up, he waved his deputy Travis Lakewood into his office. "Morning, Travis."

"Cade." He eased down in the adjacent chair on the other side of the desk. His gaze scanned his features. "Were you here all night?"

He leaned forward and tried again to straighten the papers. "Do I look bad?"

A chuckle eased past his lips and he indicated the desk with a pointed finger. "Your usual organizational skills are not in attendance this morning."

"Somewhere…" He gave up and leaned back in his chair. "I sketched out the details for the apple festival this weekend."

"Were you able to round up a few additional helpers for security?"

"Yes. I called in some extra recruits. Everything should run smoothly." He spied a piece of paper on the floor and bent to retrieve it. The schedule. He passed it to his deputy. "We may even have some downtime to enjoy some of the festivities ourselves."

"Great." He scanned the list and handed it back. "Looks good." He slapped his leg. "Oh, hey. I'm sorry. I forgot to ask. How's Riley feeling?"

"My mom took her yesterday afternoon to see Dr. Sparks. She has an ear infection." He rose from his chair and reached for his hat. "She's already made me promise she can still attend the dance Saturday night."

"Uh-oh. Does she have her eye on a boy?"

He paused in placing his hat on his head as a shiver shook him. A boy? His daughter's teenage years were upon him whether he was ready or not.

Travis laughed and rose as well. "Someone has the dad in the headlights look."

He swallowed hard. "Is it obvious?"

"Maybe." Travis chuckled and shook his head. "Don't let Riley know you aren't in command of the situation."

"Speaking of control. Did you know your grandmother called the station last night?"

"No." He frowned in concern. "Is she all right?"

"You haven't spoken to her this morning?" At his negative shake he continued, "Dispatch received the call as I was about to head home."

"Were Clive's cattle out again and roaming her apple orchard?"

He shook his head and chuckled. "You're going to wish you had taken this call."

"What did my grandmother do now?"

"One of Clara's friends, Cora Scott, is visiting with her granddaughter. Cora convinced Sierra to go skinny-dipping in the pond down the hill from your grandmother's place. Then she absconded with Sierra's clothes."

His deputy's mouth opened and closed a couple of times before he stammered, "How old is the granddaughter?"

"I didn't catch her age, but she's an adult."

A devilish grin appeared upon Travis' face. "No way."

"Hey. Is my imagination good enough to make this type of scenario up?" He waved a hand and continued, "Clara called in a disturbance and when I arrived, Sierra Scott was cowering behind a tree. With nothing on but her birthday suit."

Travis' mouth hitched a few more times before he repeated, "No way."

"Want to hear the clincher?"

All he could do was nod his head.

Cade continued at his prolonged silence. "I think Clara and her friend were matchmaking."

"Huh? You and this Sierra?"

He chuckled again as he remembered her comment about using his handcuffs. "No. I was the innocent bystander." Another chuckle rumbled past his lips. "Fair warning. I think your grandmother is trying to set you up…again." He finished placing his hat on his head. "I'm going to the fairgrounds to check on how the vendor setup is going." He picked his keys up off the desk. "Call if you need me."

Chapter Four

Silence greeted Sierra the next morning as she left her room. A feeling of foreboding traveled down her spine as she closed the bedroom door and made her way to the kitchen. That was where she found the conspiring duo with their heads together, whispering to each other. Dread on an empty stomach wasn't always a good thing. "Please tell me you're not plotting against me this early in the morning. My defenses aren't awake." The two sprung apart as she retrieved a coffee mug from the cabinet. No sign of guilt apparent upon their faces. Boy, they were good.

"Good morning, honey. How did you sleep?"

She poured a dollop of creamer into her coffee and stirred while keeping a watchful eye on Gram and Clara. Yep. Something was up. Gram wasn't a morning person and there was just a little too much pep in her voice. She squinted over the rim of her cup. "Like a baby. I guess the swim last night must have worn me out."

Cora crossed over to pat her on the back. "Like I always say…exercise is good for the body and soul."

She almost choked on the sip she'd taken. "I was being sarcastic, Gram." Leaning back against the counter she took another sip before asking, "Am I going to be privy to today's schedule?"

Her facial expression didn't give anything away. "Why wouldn't we tell you what we have planned for the day?"

Why indeed? Since her grandmother had walked into her office the previous morning, Sierra's control over anything was non-existent. She shrugged her shoulders. "No reason." Her sarcasm was once again lost in translation as Gram continued as if she hadn't spoken.

"Clara sets up her booth at the fairgrounds today for the apple festival. Would you like to help?"

She glanced at Clara. "What type of items do you sell?"

"Apple butter." She opened a cabinet and brought out a jar. "Want to try a taste?"

She accepted a spoon from Clara and took a bite. The spices bursting upon her tongue surprised her. This wasn't like any apple butter she'd sampled before. "Wow. Clara. This is delicious." Her mind automatically whirled to how the product could be marketed and sold. "Have you thought about selling this on a larger scale?"

Gram chuckled and emptied the remains of her coffee cup into the sink. "See. Sierra is always thinking about how to make a profit. She got the ability from her grandfather."

"Sorry, Clara." Warmth flooded her cheeks. "I guess I don't know how to shut it off. Even when I'm supposed to be on vacation."

"That's okay, dear." She replaced the lid on the container. "You're not the only one who has propositioned me for the recipe or wanted to sell it on a bigger platform." Once she replaced the jar in the cabinet she continued, "It's an old family recipe handed down for generations. No offense, but it's going to stay in the family."

"Well. Let me know if you change your mind." She

smiled and winked. "I have connections." The last drop of coffee had cooled, and she rinsed her cup and placed it in the dishwasher. "I'll be ready to go as soon as I check in with Janet at the office."

Gram and Clara exchanged a glance. "Take your time, dear."

The look passing between them once again caused her to worry. When Gram said she would have to be on her toes, she wasn't kidding. Her assistant answered on the first ring but whispered her greeting. "Can you hang on a moment?"

"Is something wrong?" Her question was met with silence. What crisis was the office in already? Anxiety scooted up her spine. She'd known better. This impromptu vacation shouldn't have happened until after the expansion was finished.

The moments ticked by at a snail's pace. She caught herself biting a thumbnail before she wrenched it away.

"Sierra? I'm back. Are you having fun on vacation?"

Lost in her panic, she hadn't heard Janet come back on the line. Her words sunk in. Was she having fun? Would her assistant be so blasé if there were problems at the office? She tried to take a calming breath. "I'm trying to contain the alarm coursing through my body because you put me on hold. Please tell me everything is fine there at the office."

"There isn't a thing wrong, boss. We've got this."

Her assurance chased away her panic. "There isn't anything I need to handle?"

"Try to contain your shock." There was a moment of silence before she continued, "Mr. Dunham stopped by. He was here when you called. I'm gathering from his visit you hadn't told him you were leaving town. Should

I have let you talk to him?"

Michael had stopped by the office? She hoped it was for business and not another attempt to ask her out. "Did you tell him I'm out of town?"

A chuckle sounded over the cell. "Not exactly. I told him you weren't available. He would like for you to call him."

She'd noticed a missed call the previous evening but had chosen not to give him a call back. "How did he seem?"

"A little irritated. But we both know that's his normal."

She smiled at her assistant's words. Was everyone anti-Michael? "I'll see if I have any time this afternoon to give him a call, but if he's calling about business, he needs to reach out to Mark since I left him in charge." She cradled the phone to her ear as she pulled a T-shirt from the dresser. "And? Anything else I need to know about?"

"There isn't anything at the moment. I haven't received the mail yet this morning. I'm still on the lookout for the documents from Mr. Stevens regarding the fall gala."

She held her phone out and tugged her shirt over her head before continuing, "Sounds like you have everything under control. I appreciate your extra help."

"You needed these days off. If Cora wouldn't have wrestled you into taking some time off, I would have found a way to make you take a break."

"Thanks, Janet." She paused in disconnecting. "Call if you need me."

****

Sierra groaned as she swiped at a trail of sweat

beading her brow. She'd gotten soft in the comforts of her office at Scott Enterprises. This morning's hard work had felt good. A glance about showed what Gram, Clara, and herself had accomplished. Clara's booth looked fabulous.

"That's it." Approval lit Clara's features. "I think we're ready for the festivities to start this weekend." She eased herself in between them and put an arm around her and Gram's waists. "Thank you both for coming to help."

Cora gave her friend a squeeze. "Since we've got this task out of the way, it's time for me to treat you to a hamburger and shake."

Sierra frowned at her grandmother. "Am I not invited?"

She chuckled and bent to pick up her purse. "Of course, dear. I thought you'd like to have some time to yourself and explore Harts Valley on your own."

Wasn't the whole purpose of this trip with Gram to spend time with each other? Now she seemed to be banishing her. "All right, Gram. Go ahead and have your secrets. I'll meet you back at Clara's house later this afternoon." The two friends left with their heads pressed together.

Her cell jangled inside her pocket. She smiled as her sister's name appeared on the caller ID. "Hey, Em. What's up?"

"I got off the phone with your office. I couldn't believe my ears when your assistant said you were on vacation. Was she telling the truth?"

She chuckled, grabbed a nearby chair, and sat. "Can you believe it? Gram talked me into taking a few weeks off."

"Wow. I've been trying for months to get you to slow down. Remind me to thank Gram."

She frowned at her sister's teasing. Had her whole family been worried about her? Maybe once the expansion was complete, she would reevaluate her work life ratio. "You'll never guess what Gram and her friend Clara did to me last night."

"Does it beat the time she talked me into a hot dog costume at a baseball game?"

She tapped her fingers on her knee. "I have you beat. She's getting craftier in her old age."

"I'll be the judge. What did she do?"

She took a few moments to relay the details of her skinny-dipping escapade to her sister. A stunned silence followed once she finished. "Em? You still there?"

"Holy cow." A snuffle escaped before her sister dissolved into laughter. "You're right. Your saga beats my horror story by a long shot."

She found herself joining in her merriment. "And this is only day two of my vacation."

"You are so in trouble."

"Hey. I appreciate you checking in, but I'm going to let you go. I'm going to tour Harts Valley."

"Have fun with Gram. Give her a hug from me." Emily snickered. "Let me know what other antics she throws your way."

She smiled as she disconnected the call. Gram was an equal opportunity instigator. Emily's time was coming. No grandchild would be spared the ministrations of her matchmaking.

A glance about proved most of the vendors had left the building while she'd been on her call. She frowned as she searched for her purse. Where had she placed it?

N. Jade Gray

She'd brought it in. Hadn't she? Hands on hips she turned slowly. The only logical place left to look was the Jeep.

A slight breeze greeted her as she exited the building. She wrenched the driver's side door handle, but it didn't budge. She cupped her hands and gazed into the cab. Her purse and keys lay on the passenger seat. She sprinted around the vehicle and checked all the doors. Each was locked. Great.

"Problem?"

A squeal escaped as she spun about. Her hand flew to her racing heart as her gaze met the sheriff's who stood a few feet away. "Sheriff. I swear you live for finding me in the worse situations."

He shrugged and his lips quirked in a crooked grin. "Well, my job is to find trouble."

"That it is." She chuckled and swiped at a wisp of hair blowing into her eyes.

"Surely you aren't out here working on your tan?"

"No sir." She pointed to the window. "Funny thing. It seems I've locked myself out of my Jeep."

He crossed the remaining distance and leaned over to glance inside.

She sniffed in appreciation of his masculine scent. What was she doing? With a shake of her head, she tried to focus on her current problem. "Any chance you would be able to open the door?"

He frowned and shook his head. "Not for this newer model. I'll call Frank at the service shop in town. Why don't we phone from inside?"

She almost wrenched her arm out of the socket when the door to the building she recently vacated didn't budge. Locked? Really? She turned and shrugged. "Next idea?"

He knocked on the door and waited a few seconds. No one answered their summons. "Let's sit in my vehicle."

She hadn't noticed the patrol car sitting a few feet away. He opened the door for her and she quickly slid in. A glance down at her white T-shirt made her cringe. Several streaks of dirt decorated the front. She always seemed to be at her worst around this man.

His gaze did a quick sweep of her frame as he slid into the driver's seat before he retrieved the cell lying on the dash.

Minutes later he ended his call. "Good news. Frank can help unlock your vehicle. The bad news is he had a call for a tow out of town. It may be about an hour or more before he can assist you."

She leaned her head back, turned her head, and met his gaze.

"You hungry?"

Her stomach responded with a resounding rumble. His lips quirked before he put the keys in the ignition and started the car. "Betsy's Café downtown has it all."

"Oh." She glanced at her Jeep. "I don't have my wallet."

"Don't worry about it. My treat."

Even though he said not to fret over his offer, she still felt like a free loader. He maneuvered the vehicle a moment before she asked, "I'm not taking you away from any of your duties, am I?"

"Right now, I'm helping a damsel in distress." His gaze met hers again as he smiled. "I believe that falls under my job description."

Her phone trilled in her pocket. She answered on the

third ring. "Hi, Gram."

"Have you left the fairgrounds?"

"Not really." A tremble of unease ran down her spine. "Why?"

There was a small pause before she answered, "Oh, no reason, dear." There was mumbling in the background before she continued, "I wanted to know if you needed help with anything."

The trepidation she'd experienced moments before doubled. A disturbing thought edged into her brain. Surely her grandmother wouldn't have locked her out of her vehicle. Was the idea a little far-fetched? Wasn't it? "I'm good. I'll meet up with you later."

"Well." An awkward silence bounced off her ear. "Okay, dear. If you're sure you don't need any help."

The mystery of the locked Jeep was solved. The dynamic duo had struck again. She could see the scenario playing in her mind. She shook her head in wonder. "I'm fine, Gram. I'm going to grab some lunch." A snicker escaped as her grandmother harrumphed before she ended the call. "Those women are going to help pay for the service call to unlock my vehicle. I know they locked my keys in my Jeep. On purpose."

The sheriff's brow hitched. "Should I try to guess why?"

"If you haven't caught on, Gram and Clara are trying their hand at matchmaking." She turned farther in her seat until she faced him. "Let me set the scene for you. I panic when I find my keys and purse locked in my vehicle. I call Gram for help and poof a young deputy, Travis, Clara's grandson, arrives like a knight in shining armor to save me."

"You think they'd go to such great lengths?" He

shrugged his shoulders in disbelief.

"Hello." She tapped a finger to her forehead. "Remember how you found me last night?"

A deep chuckle rumbled in his chest. "Right. You may have a point."

"I know I do." She crossed her arms and turned to stare out the passenger window.

"Why are Cora and Clara going to such extremes?"

Why indeed? "I made the mistake of telling Gram a man she doesn't like wants to date me." Her gaze dropped from his dark brown eyes. She was sure her grandmother wouldn't have approved of her sitting here with a near stranger getting breathless from his nearness either. Which situation was worse? She splayed her hands. "Anyway, Gram wasn't a fan of his to begin with…"

"Thus, the interference."

Her gaze connected with his amused one. "Now you're catching on."

Chapter Five

The lunch crowd was beginning to arrive at Betsy's Café by the time Cade pulled the car into the parking lot. "Have you visited Harts Valley before?"

"No. This is my first visit." She looked out the side window. "What I have seen of the town so far looks quaint. I hope to tour downtown this afternoon." She paused and bit her lip. "After I get my Jeep unlocked, of course."

"My mother-in-law has a boutique a block from here. Across from the courthouse." He pulled the keys from the ignition and reached for the door handle. "If you need a little retail therapy."

Her chuckle floated on the slight breeze as she exited and met him in front of the car. "Sounds like the voice of experience."

"I'm surrounded by the opposite sex in my household." He lifted his shoulders in a shrug. "I've learned to know when a female needs to hit the shops." As his hand rested on her lower back for her to precede him into the café, an alluring warmth spread from his palm to his fingertips. An irresistible fragrance clung to her body and teased his nose. When was the last time he'd noticed a woman's scent? Whether artificial or natural?

"Hey, Sheriff. Find an empty spot and I'll be with you shortly."

With a shake of his head, he shook off his musings. "Thanks, Betsy." A table was available in the middle of the room, and he guided Sierra toward it and pulled out a chair for her.

Her eyes roamed over the other occupants before her gaze connected with his. "Best kind of advertisement is a booming business." She pulled out a menu from behind the napkin holder and began to examine the offerings. "What do you recommend?"

Before he could answer, Betsy stopped by the table with a tablet in her hand.

"Cade, have you had your daily limit of coffee yet?"

"Not quite. Why don't you bring me a cup with a glass of water?"

"Sure thing." She turned and studied the woman sitting across from him. "What can I get for you, miss?"

"I think I will have a lemonade."

Cade could tell Betsy was curious about his companion but was restraining from asking a multitude of questions. He hid a smile behind a raised hand. The rumor mill would be going wild in less than thirty minutes.

Betsy tilted her head and tapped her pencil against her lips. "Do I know you from somewhere?"

He inwardly groaned. So much in believing the other woman had restraint. His gaze shifted to Sierra. A blush made its way up her neck and crept toward her cheeks. Was she thinking he'd ratted her out about the pond incident the night before? He frowned. The small town had a way of knowing when things happened.

"Maybe I have one of those faces?" A nervous laugh accompanied her question.

The waitress studied her a bit longer before she said,

"I'll be right back with your drinks."

The radio attached to his belt squawked and he turned down the volume. He took a moment to study her as she looked over the food choices. She wore her chestnut hair up in one of those scrunchy things Riley liked to leave lying around the house. From what he could tell she hadn't bothered putting on makeup. Her gaze locked with his. He pointed at the menu. "Would you like my recommendation?"

She folded the menu and placed it back behind the napkin holder. "What do you suggest?"

"You can't go wrong with anything here, but I'm partial to the mushroom Swiss burger."

"Hmmm." She glanced about at the other tables before asking, "How about the onion rings?"

He could practically see her salivating before his eyes. A smile tugged at his lips before he threw a wink in her direction. "You won't be disappointed."

Betsy appeared by their table and placed their drinks in front of them. "What can I get started for you?"

After they relayed their order, he settled back in his chair. "So, Sierra. Where are you from?" He caught a slight hesitation before she answered.

"Born and raised in Oklahoma. Currently, I live in the Tulsa area." She took a sip of her lemonade. "How about you?"

"Originally, I'm from Texas. I attended college in Oklahoma"—he shrugged his shoulders—"and never left."

"Uh-oh." A teasing glint appeared in her eyes. "A Texan? Where does your allegiance lie? Which Oklahoma university did you attend?"

"Does it matter?"

"Maybe." She leaned in and whispered, "Crimson and Cream or Orange and Black?"

The college rivalry was serious business in most states and Oklahoma wasn't any different. Her direct stare almost made him squirm. Betsy saved him from answering by placing their food on the table. She asked him to pass the ketchup bottle and squirted some on her plate.

A fat onion ring poised in her fingers was pointed in his direction. "This conversation isn't over."

As far as he was concerned the discussion was closed. He took a bite before he chose to broach a change in subject. "What were you doing at the fairgrounds?"

"We were helping Clara set up her booth for the festival. Have you tried her apple butter?"

"Sure." He wiped his mouth with a napkin. "It's legendary in these parts."

"I tried to convince her this morning she needs to sell on a bigger scale."

He tilted his head. "I'm guessing you got shot down."

"Got it in one. But I'll probably keep bugging until I wear her down."

"How long are you in town?" The question was more than curiosity on his part. He waved a hand. "You know. How much time do you have to wear her down?"

"I'm taking a two week break from work. This trip was a spontaneous vacation." She sighed and shrugged. "Another one of Gram's accomplishments over the last few days."

"What is it you do for a living?" His cell vibrated and interrupted her answer. "Excuse me." He rose from the table. "It's dispatch. I've got to take this." A few steps from the table he answered, "Hi, Wendy." He listened a moment before he turned his head to slant a look back at Sierra. "Not necessary. I know exactly where Sierra Scott is. You can reassure her grandmother she hasn't been kidnapped. I'll be back in the office shortly. Thanks."

Sierra put her forehead into her hands and leaned on the table. She didn't look him in the eye as he sat back down. "Let me guess…Gram." She peeked at him through her fingers before reaching to pull her cell from her back pocket. "Oh no. I have three missed calls from her." Pushing the button on the side to turn up the volume, she mumbled, "Sorry. I didn't hear my phone ring."

"You got it in one." He smiled and shook his head. "Cora called my office worrying you'd been kidnapped."

A groan emerged. "I'm so sorry. I guess I should get back to my Jeep before I cause any more problems for you."

He waved a hand at the meal in front of them. "No hurry. Let's finish our food. No need to waste those tasty onion rings."

Her lips tilted into a smile. "You make a valid point, Sheriff."

They finished their meal and he rose and placed his hat on his head. "I'll drive you back." When they arrived back at the fairgrounds, Frank already had her Jeep door open. Cade watched Sierra banter with the locksmith. He needed to get back to the office, but he was enjoying her company. She was a breath of fresh air in his stale world. Had he stopped enjoying life? Except for his daughter and job, he'd shut out so much. Sierra made him feel alive and something more than a dad or sheriff. And the feeling hadn't happened in a long time.

"Thanks again, Sheriff, for the bail out and the lunch. I appreciate your help. I'd love to say I won't cause any more problems for you while I'm in town, but when I'm hanging with Gram, I can't promise you anything."

With a wave of her hand, she climbed into her vehicle and drove away. He found himself whistling softly as he made his way back to his own car and driving back to the office.

Chapter Six

A glance in her rearview proved the sheriff watched as she drove away. What could he be thinking? Was he keeping an eye on her because she seemed certifiably nuts? Sierra pushed the phone button on her steering wheel and waited for her call to connect. A sigh of relief was the first thing she heard as her grandmother answered.

"Where have you been?"

"Sorry, Gram. I didn't hear my phone ring."

"Where on Earth have you been? You aged me a couple of years, young lady. I thought something bad had happened. I worry about those things you know."

A deep inhale sounded through the speaker. "Gram. Are you hyperventilating?"

"Not anymore." A loud exhale leaked from her lungs before she continued, "I called the police when you didn't answer."

"I know."

"What do you mean?" Her infuriated huff echoed throughout the cab. "You know?"

"Cade told me."

Her grandmother was silent for a moment. "Cade? Who's Cade?"

Even as irritated as Gram was at the moment, Sierra could practically hear the wheels turning in her head at the mention of a man's name.

"The sheriff, Cade Collins. You met him last night."

"Oh."

"Sorry, Gram." She almost felt sorry for her grandmother. The mission to find her a man other than Michael Dunham wasn't going so well. "No matchmaking opportunity for you."

She sputtered in frustration, "I wasn't thinking such a thing."

Liar, her mind screamed.

"Sierra?"

"Sorry. I'm driving and trying to pay attention to what I'm doing." Was lightning going to strike at the fib?

"Driving? In your Jeep?"

Should she bring up the fact Gram had intentionally locked her purse and keys in the vehicle? Would the attempt to berate her make any difference? She'd lucked out when Frank didn't charge her for unlocking the Jeep. He'd owed Cade a favor. The debt of gratitude was piling up. How was she going to repay the sheriff's kindness? He said he'd been doing his job, but she believed she owed him.

"Sierra? Are you on your way back to the house?"

A car backed out on the main street, and she eased in to park. The courthouse reflected in her rearview as she pushed off the ignition. "No, Grams. I'm downtown. I'm going to check out some of these cute shops here on the square. Indulge in some retail therapy."

"Well, thank you for checking in with me. When I didn't hear from you right away my vivid imagination took flight. Have fun shopping. Let us know when you are heading back to the house."

"I will." She made sure her keys were in her purse before she zipped it shut. "Gram. I promise my ringer on

my cell is now set on full blast."
****
"Dad."

Cade put down his pen and smiled as Riley dashed into his office. "Hey there." He noted her face wasn't as pale as the day before. The antibiotic for the ear infection must have kicked in. "You look like you feel better."

"Tons." She plopped down in an office chair.

"How was school?"

"Ken Darby puked at lunch." She shuddered. "I almost hurled myself."

"I'm glad you have an iron stomach." His chair squeaked as he leaned back. "How did you do on your science test?" A shoulder shrug along with an eye roll made him smile.

"Dunno."

He lifted a brow. "That's all you got?"

"Mr. Thomas will grade them tonight." She nibbled her lip a moment. "Can I go shopping at Nanny's store before we head home?"

He flicked his wrist and glanced at the time. Three thirty. "I don't see why not, but what are you shopping for?"

An invisible piece of lint seemed to catch her attention before she answered. "Something for the dance this weekend."

Travis' words from this morning about Riley liking a boy danced in his head. His deputy seemed more in tune with his daughter than he seemed to be. He rose and picked up his hat.

A look of panic crossed her features. "You don't have to go with me."

There was no way he'd let her go shopping

unaccompanied. Her idea of appropriate attire and his hadn't meshed lately. "I'd feel better if I added some input."

"Dad." The irritation was evident in her tone. "Allison's dad didn't help her with what she's wearing to the dance."

He folded his arms across his chest. "But I'm sure Allison's mom did."

A huff left her lips as she preceded him out of his office. "I guess." Her shoulders drooped as if he was escorting her to the guillotine. "Let's get this over with."

The silence a prisoner exhibited while riding in his patrol car couldn't compare to his daughter's silent treatment. She would have won hands down. He glanced over and opened his mouth to make conversation, but snapped it shut again at the look on her face. A memory popped into his head where Melissa, Riley's mom, had worn the same expression. Now probably wasn't the time to tell her she looked like her mom.

The bell above the door at The Sunshine Boutique announced their entrance. A frustrated sigh escaped from his daughter. "What's wrong?"

"Nanny's not here."

He glanced over to see Sonya Campbell standing by the cash register. "Hi, Sonya. Is Mary here?"

"Hi, Cade. Riley." She shook her head. "Did she know you were coming by?"

"No."

"She had some errands she needed to run before she went home. I'm closing the store tonight. Is there anything I can help you with?"

Sonya gave him a quick perusal from his head to his feet. Did he read her wrong? Was the look one of appreciation? He shook his head. What was going on with him lately? "Riley wanted help picking out something appropriate for the apple festival dance."

"I'd be glad to help."

"Dad."

It was said under her breath, but the word was laced with frustration. Obviously, he was still too uncouth to help with young lady's apparel.

"Here for a little retail therapy, Sheriff?"

A small thrill trekked through his body. He'd not heard Sierra approach. His gaze swung to where she stood a few feet away.

"Are you following me?" Her hazel eyes sparkled back at him in amusement.

A low chuckle escaped. "No, Miss Scott. But maybe I should ask you the same thing."

"I saw you come into the store." She held out a folded wool blanket. "I forgot to give this to you earlier when you rode to my rescue…once again."

He accepted the blanket with thoughts of the previous night coming back to him in vivid color.

"I thought you may need it back for the next damsel you need to rescue."

A throat clearing brought Cade's attention back to his daughter as she looked from him to Miss Scott. "Oh. Sorry." He placed an arm around Riley's shoulder. "This is my daughter Riley."

"Hi, Riley. I'm Sierra Scott."

A peculiar look came over his daughter's face before she asked, "Are you a friend of my dad?"

"I guess." A look of uncertainty crossed her features.

Cade watched as a myriad of expressions crossed his

daughter's face. She was about to suggest something he wasn't going to like.

"Dad. Can Sierra help me find my dress?"

Yup. He'd nailed it. Riley was trying to ditch him. "I thought Sonya and I were going to help you." He made a last attempt to retain the other clerk's help. Sonya looked at him and motioned to another customer who entered the store. He was losing ground fast.

Sierra tried to hide a smile as she witnessed Cade struggling to remain in control of the situation and his daughter. Where was his wife in this shopping crisis scenario? "Is there something special you're looking for, Riley?"

"Yes. I want a new dress for the dance this weekend."

From the corner of her eye, she caught Cade sweeping his cowboy hat off his head and running a hand through his hair. His gaze lacked its usual merriment when she met his look. "I'd love to help. Head over to the junior section and I'll join you after I have a word with your dad."

She gave an enthusiastic nod. "See you, Dad. I'll let you know when we're done, if you want to head back to the station."

Sierra grinned as she watched Riley practically float across the floor. Noting his concerned glance she asked, "Do you trust me?"

"The verdict is still out."

She laughed at the seriousness of his words. "How old is Riley?"

His hand made another pass through his hair. "Fifteen going on thirty."

"Let me guess. She wants an outfit to draw the

45

attention of a certain boy."

Fright crossed his features. "Oh Lord, help me."

She placed a hand on his arm and he tensed at her touch. "Hey. It's okay. I can help steer her in the right direction."

"Boys." A gurgling noise seeped from his lips. "I'm not ready for this."

It wasn't polite to make fun of the grown man having a panic attack, but his actions were endearing. "Is your wife at work and not able to help her shop today?"

A far away expression clouded his features for a moment. "I'm sure she would have loved to." His dark brown eyes snagged her gaze. "My wife passed about five years ago."

Way to go, Sierra. Stick your foot into your mouth. "I'm sorry. I didn't know." She squared her shoulders and looked back over at Riley. She was holding a red strapless dress up against her body. Cade saw what she held and another groan emerged. "Okay. I've got this. You're going to have to trust me." She patted his arm to get his attention. "Give me your phone number and I will call when we are done."

Chapter Seven

Sierra gazed at Cade's retreating back. He hadn't wanted to leave, but she finally convinced him to trust her with his daughter's clothing selection. And his credit card.

Riley's gaze met hers in the reflection of the mirror in front of her. The red strapless dress still clasped against her body. She swung about with excitement upon her face. "What do you think?"

This was going to take a little finesse. Maybe even more skill than brokering a multi-million-dollar deal. She tapped a finger to her lips. "First. What's the name of the boy you like?"

She glanced around. "Did Dad leave?"

"Yes. I sent him packing." Uncertainty still lingered upon the teenager's face. "I promise I won't tell." She made a cross symbol over her heart. "If you don't want me to."

She leaned forward and whispered, "Noah Spencer."

"Okay. Tell me a little about Noah."

The girl's cheeks turned rosy. "He's sixteen and I sit behind him in science class."

"Let me see if I understand the situation. You like him. But you don't know if he knows you exist." She turned and took the red dress out of her hands and held it up. "Thus, you want to dress in something to make him notice you. Tell me if I'm off base here."

"Yes." A look of awe settled on the girl's face. "How did you know?"

She placed an arm around her waist and gave her a light squeeze. "I've been there, done that. But I'm going to ask you something and I need you to be honest with me." The teenager nodded and Sierra turned her back around to face the mirror. "Here." She gave the dress back to her. "Hold it back up." After Riley did so, she asked, "Do you think you will feel comfortable wearing this outfit?"

Her dark eyes wavered as she looked down. "No."

"Did you choose this one in hopes of capturing Noah's attention?"

She gave a slight nod. "Yes. How did you know?"

Sierra placed a finger under her chin and smiled as her gaze finally met hers. "It's a tale as old as time." She took the dress from her grasp and hung it on a nearby rack. "What are you comfortable wearing?"

"The truth?" She glanced down at her blue jeans and sneakers. "This is what makes me comfortable."

"Okay. I can work with this." She went to another rack and started going from hanger to hanger. "What type of boy is Noah?"

She tilted her head. "What do you mean?"

"Is he quiet? Studious? Loud? Boisterous?" She waved a hand in the air. "You know. What makes Noah…Noah?"

A smile appeared on her face and the gesture made her eyes twinkle. A trait she had in common with her dad. "He's quiet. Studious. I like his quirky grin."

"What else?"

"I think he's a hard worker. His family owns a ranch

outside of town. They raise cattle and horses."

"Ah-ha." She snapped her fingers. "Now we're getting somewhere. Do you feel he's a cowboy in the making?"

A girlish giggle escaped as she nodded. "Yes."

"Are you sure he'll be at the dance?"

"Positive." Her lips firmed with purpose. "I overheard his friend Tanner ask him if he was going."

The peal of one of her favorite tunes interrupted them. She pulled her cell from her purse and frowned. Michael was calling. She'd forgotten to call him back. A press of her finger to the side of the phone silenced it.

"Do you need to answer that?"

"I'll call him back in a minute." She bit her lip and brought her focus back to the matter at hand. "Do you have a pair of cowboy boots?"

"Yeah." Her shoulder shrug indicated her question was silly. "I do. But they're kind of ratty."

"Wait a moment. Hold that thought. I have an idea." She pulled up Cade's number on her phone. "Hi, Cade. Is it okay to take Riley down to the western store after we finish here to buy a pair of new boots?"

Silence greeted her for a moment. "Riley wants boots?"

A chuckle slipped out at his confusion. "Are you losing trust in my capabilities so soon?"

"I hope I don't regret this, but you have my credit card."

"And I'm not afraid to use it." She hung up before he had a chance to change his mind. A smile still rested on her lips as she presented a pale green dress with short sleeves and scooped neck to Riley. "What do you think about this one?"

"Are you sure?" Her brow furrowed. "Will Noah like it?"

The father and daughter shared a common trait. They didn't trust her opinion. She shook her head and handed the garment to her. "Why don't you try it on? I'll look for a jacket to put with it." She smiled as Riley headed for the dressing room. It was fun helping the teen.

Her phone vibrated in her hand. A new voicemail. She listened to yet another of Michael's messages before she returned his call. When he answered she said, "I'm sorry. I meant to call you back earlier."

"I was beginning to wonder if you're avoiding me."

His cool tone conveyed his displeasure. "No. Not at all. I've been busy."

"I stopped by your office today with some papers for you to sign and to ask if you would like to attend a firm dinner meeting with me on Thursday. I'd hoped you could go with me."

Another invitation. She sighed and rubbed her temple. "I'm sorry, Michael. I can't."

"Can't? Or won't?"

The tone of his voice indicated he was agitated. Had he always been this whiney? "I can't because I'll be out of town."

"Out of town? Where you going?"

Was it the attorney's business where she was? "Actually. I'm already out of town. Mark Simons is handling matters at the office while I'm away. He can look over the paperwork you dropped off earlier."

There was a pause before he asked, "How long are you going to be gone?"

Did she hear him grind his teeth? "Mark should be able to handle any matters for me while I'm away."

"What about the expansion project? Are you blowing it off?"

Irritation bubbled in her stomach. In an attempt to calm her exasperation, she took a steadying breath, unclenched her fist, and counted to three. "No. I'm not blowing it off. Mark is handling the final matters. Everything is fine."

"As your attorney, I wish you had made me aware of this development."

Was it too late to request different counsel? A sigh emerged and she didn't try to cover her frustration. She glanced up to see Riley emerge from the dressing room with a huge smile upon her face. "I've got to go, Mr. Dunham. I'll see you when I'm back in town." She hung up on his sputtering reply. "Come here and let me look at you."

She twirled in front of the mirror. "I love it."

Her phone began to ring instantly and she silenced it before holding out a dark green jacket. "Try this on to see how it looks with the dress." She stood behind her as she shrugged into the coat. Riley's gaze met hers in the reflection. "Do you feel comfy in the dress?" At her nod she continued. "Something to remember when shopping. You want to feel comfortable in what you're wearing. If you don't, then you won't feel relaxed when you want to speak to a certain boy."

"Thank you, Sierra."

"Now. Let's go spend some more of your dad's money and grab you a new pair of boots."

****

Cade glanced again at his watch. What could be taking so long? He'd expected them back by now. A sigh escaped as a giggle echoed down the hall. Riley entered his office moments later all smiles with Sierra trailing behind. Each held several packages and they placed them in one of his office chairs. "I see retail therapy was a success."

"Dad. Wait till you see the dress Sierra helped pick out. I love it."

His gaze met Sierra's. The warmth and amusement lighting her gaze made his pulse leap. His heart skipped a beat and sputtered as she winked. He swallowed as he tried to relieve the dryness in residence inside his mouth. "I can't wait for you to show me."

Riley turned to her. "Thank you again for your help."

"You're welcome."

He stood behind his desk, forgotten as Riley gave Sierra a grateful hug.

She leaned back and asked, "Are you going to the dance?"

A frown marred Sierra's brow. "I hadn't thought about it."

"You've got to. It's going to be so much fun. Besides." She cut a quick glance in his direction. "I need your help on how to talk to Noah."

Cade tried not to let his shock show. There was a boy and his name was Noah. He caught Sierra's small shake of her head. Was she trying to silently tell him not to go into panic mode for the second time today? He skirted his desk and retrieved his hat. "Thank you again for your help with Riley's purchases."

She opened her purse, retrieved his credit card, and held it out to him. "It was my pleasure."

He pocketed the card before grabbing a couple of the nearby shopping bags. "Riley, I need to cover a shift tonight. Do you want me to drop you off at home or Nanny's house?"

"Nanny's. I want to show her my new outfit." She flung her arms around Sierra to give her another quick hug. "Night, Sierra."

They followed the giddy teenager from the station. He stopped on the sidewalk and met her gaze. "I'll wait to make sure your Jeep starts."

She nodded and smiled. "Thanks. I'll see you around, Sheriff."

Without a backwards glance, she climbed into her vehicle and started it up. He called out, "Good night" before she gave them a final wave and backed away.

Chapter Eight

The afternoon of shopping had felt good. Sierra sat a moment at a nearby traffic light and glanced into her rearview mirror before continuing on when the light turned green. Cade and Riley pulled in behind her, but turned at the intersection and were out of sight within moments. How long had it been since she'd enjoyed a day without worrying about paperwork or meetings? A contented sigh escaped. Far too long.

At the next stop, she pulled her phone from her purse and quickly sent a text to Gram letting her know she was heading back to Clara's house. Now wasn't the time to test the theory that Gram would call out the National Guard if she didn't know her eta. How embarrassing would it be to have the sheriff's office called back out again?

Her thoughts turned to the phone conversation with attorney Michael Dunham. She frowned at his assumption she was blowing off her responsibilities. Who was he to dictate how she spent her time?

The sun was sinking as she pulled into the drive and parked in front of Clara's. A tantalizing aroma greeted her as she opened the door. Something smelled delicious. She entered the kitchen to find Gram and Clara setting the table. "Whatever you've got in the oven smells like heaven."

"We made lasagna." Gram finished placing a dish

on the table. "I hope you're hungry."

"I am." She held up a couple of bags. "Shopping works up an appetite."

A look of confusion crossed her features before frown lines marred her forehead. "You were gone all afternoon and three bags are the only purchases you have to show for it?"

"Oh. Trust me. I got a workout. I helped Riley with her purchases for the dance this weekend."

"Riley?" She placed her hands on her hips. "Do I know her?"

"That is Sheriff Collins' teenage daughter." She turned to exit the kitchen. "I'll wash up and be back shortly.

Cora watched her granddaughter walk from the room. Over the last couple of days Sierra had spent quite a bit of time in the company of the sheriff.

"Cora?" Clara stood by the stove with a look of bewilderment upon her face. "What's the matter?"

"Hmmm."

She put the potholders on the counter. "What does hmmm mean? You've got a strange look on your face."

Cora nodded but didn't answer her question.

She glanced about and whispered, "Do you think she suspects we locked her keys in her Jeep?"

"She hasn't brought up the incident." Cora shook her head. "Which means she knows what we did and is choosing not to confront us."

Surprise crossed her friend's face. "Did her attitude seem odd? I thought for sure she'd ream us."

She tapped a finger to her lips. "I know she knows. Which makes me wonder why she hasn't read us the riot act."

"I'm not sure we're ever going to succeed getting your granddaughter and my grandson together." A sigh escaped her lips.

The sheriff had derailed every attempt they'd made to get Sierra and Travis together. She tilted her head and bit her lip. The attempts at matchmaking the last couple of days replayed in her mind. "Clara? Tell me about the sheriff?"

She deposited the hot dish from the oven on the counter before asking, "What do you mean?"

Cora splayed her hands and met her gaze. "I need whatever intel you can give me."

"I can try." She shrugged her shoulders. "He's lived in Harts Valley for some time. I can't remember when exactly he moved here with his wife and daughter." She shook her head. "It was sad a few years ago when his wife passed. His in-laws, Roy and Mary, help him out with his daughter when needed."

"Ah-ha." Cora snapped her fingers. "That's it."

"What's it?"

"Plan B." She noticed the befuddled look upon Clara's face. "Is the sheriff single?"

An exasperated sigh escaped. "Weren't you paying attention? It's what I said. He's a widower."

She smiled and rubbed her hands together. "Is he dating anyone?"

"I don't believe so." Her brows drew together as if deep in thought. "Why?"

Cora shot her friend a wink. "Because I think we need to make a few adjustments to our plans."

****

The moment Cade and Riley arrived at Nanny's house his daughter disappeared and reappeared moments later wearing her new outfit. Relief traveled down his spine. The red strapless dress was nowhere in sight. She wore a pale green dress with a pair of mid-calf tan cowboy boots and a dark green jacket was flung over her shoulder. A quick twirl showed him and Mary the complete ensemble.

"What do you think? Dad? Nanny?"

"Oh, honey. You look like your momma." Mary swiped at the wetness at the corner of her eye. "Before I start dripping like a leaky watering pot, I'll go finish dinner."

I think I owe Sierra a debt of gratitude. He swallowed the lump that rose in his throat. Gone was his little girl. "You look all grown up."

"Ah, Dad. Don't go getting mushy."

"Sorry. Kiddo." He crossed the room to hug her close and put his chin on top of her head. "It's one of those sappy moments. I love you."

She was silent for a moment before whispering, "I love you too."

He leaned back and met her gaze. "Do I get to know more about this boy?"

"Depends." Her lips quirked upwards. "You don't plan on intimidating him with your uniform and gun do you?" She backed away. "I'm going to change. I need to help Nanny with dinner. I'll see you later when you get off work."

Once again, he realized how mature his daughter had become as she left the room. An ache overcame him as he realized in a few short years she'd be heading to college. Time was passing by way too quickly. Loneliness reared its ugly head. Is this why he'd been drawn to Sierra the last couple of days? Because he was lonely? He'd told himself now wasn't the time to pursue the pull of attraction he was feeling. But seeing Riley bloom before his eyes made him evaluate his own single status.

He needed to get back to the station, but paused as he pulled his cell from his pocket. Indecision warred in his brain as he paused with his fingers hovering over Sierra's phone number. Should he call her? What should he say? Maybe a text would be simpler. Keep it simple he advised himself.

—*Riley modeled her new outfit. I was elated to see it wasn't red or strapless. Thank you again for your help today.*—

Chapter Nine

Gram rinsed the dish in her hands and turned to Sierra. "Clara and I are going down to Walt's bar for the live music tonight. Do you want to go with us?"

She accepted the plate and dried it before placing it in the cabinet. Should alarm bells be clanging in her head? So far, every suggestion her grandmother had recommended on this vacation ended in an embarrassing encounter with the sheriff. But maybe she should go along to keep the dynamic duo out of trouble. The key locking incident was still fresh in her mind. She met her grandmother's unblinking gaze. "What type of music?"

A secret smile passed between the two women before they said in unison, "Karaoke."

"Excuse me?" Surely her ears were deceiving her. "You want to go sing Karaoke?"

She shrugged and exchanged another glance with her friend. "Sure. Why not? Isn't the whole purpose of Karaoke night to sing?" Her gaze swung back to sweep her from the top of her head to her feet. "Maybe you should freshen up before we go."

She peered down at her shirt and faded jeans. "What's wrong with what I'm wearing?"

"You look a little wrinkled, dear. Why don't you wear the pretty orange top I saw hanging in your wardrobe."

Had she gone through her clothes? She quirked a

brow. "Well. If you'll excuse me. I'll take a few moments to freshen up."

She shook her head as she spied the blouse Gram had indicated hanging in the closet. Someone did snoop. Should she even berate her for doing so?

On top of the dresser her cell pinged. She frowned as an unfamiliar number lit the screen. Her hand shook as she realized it came from Cade.

—*Riley modeled her new outfit. I was elated to see it wasn't red or strapless. Thank you again for your help today.*—

The message was short and sweet, but it warmed her heart. Was it crazy the way her heart leaped? The sheriff intrigued her and that hadn't happened in a long time. Was he interested in her as well? Or was he just being polite? She sent a thumbs up emoji and joined Gram and Clara in the living room.

"Can you drive, dear?"

"Sure." She shrugged into a jacket. "But I'll need you to give me directions."

Walt's sat on the outer edge of town. The building wasn't much to look at, but the parking lot was full. Business was booming and so was the sound system. Sierra carefully pocketed her keys and looped her purse over her neck. She wasn't taking any more unnecessary risks tonight. As they neared the entrance, she could hear someone attempting to sing a Shania Twain song. What had she got herself into? She followed Gram and Clara inside. The smell of musky beer greeted her nose as they crossed the threshold. There was a small dance floor and stage to the left and a long bar to the right. The noisy chatter of the clientele drowned out the singer on the stage.

Gram turned and leaned in to ask, "Want to get a drink?"

Sierra led the way and eased into a vacant spot at the bar. One of the bartenders nodded to them before he turned to deliver a beer. Gram winked at her as they both noticed the tight denims hugging his buttocks.

"What will it be, ladies?"

She looked at the indecision stamped on the faces of her comrades. "I'll have an Amaretto Sour."

They nodded and said in unison, "The same for us."

With drinks in hand, moments later they snagged a table. Sierra took a sip from her glass. The bartender needed an extra tip. Not only was he serious eye candy, but the man made a mean cocktail.

"Hey. This is good."

She laughed as Gram held up her glass. "Take it easy. They pack a punch."

"Why else do you think we brought you?" With two fingers she twirled the straw around. "You're the designated driver." The cherry was plucked from the drink and popped into her mouth. "Watch this." She proceeded in working the fruit and stem in her mouth before producing the stem tied in a knot.

"Did you tie it with your tongue?"

She nodded and chuckled. "It's a good way to condition yourself for French kissing."

Clara giggled and took another sip of her beverage.

She stared at her. Had she truly known her grandmother before this week?

"What?"

If possible, the twinkle in her eyes shone brighter. "Nothing."

Clara placed her jacket on a chair. "Let's check to

see if there are any slots still available. Come on, Cora, let's go add our names."

Gram took another healthy swallow from her glass. "I'm coming. Lead the way."

It was good to see her grandmother having such a good time with her friend. She shook her head. Now if she could only stop them from their matchmaking.

"Hello, darling. You here by your lonesome?"

An elderly gentleman with a plaid cowboy shirt and bolo tie stood next to the table. His gray hair was slicked back with a layer of gel. "Good evening." She pointed towards the stage. "My companions are checking out the song selections."

His gaze swung from her pointing finger to where she indicated. A smile spread across his features and he straightened his shoulders. "Finally. Some fillies my own age."

A chuckle emerged as she glanced around at the other occupants of the bar. He did have a point. She hadn't noticed. "Do you come here often?"

His thin shoulders lifted and eased down before his gaze swung back to hers. "Only when I'm bored, which seems to happen more and more these days."

She indicated the extra chair at the table. "Go ahead. Plant yourself. I'm sure my grandmother and her friend won't mind. Trust me, you won't be bored."

A smile lit up his face. "I don't mind if I do. Thanks."

"Well. Hello there." Gram eased into her seat and smiled at the newcomer. Her bracelets jangled as she offered a hand. "I'm Cora Scott. And this is my good friend Clara Lakewood. What's your name?"

"Butch Nix. But my friends call me Nix."

"Nice to meet you. Do you plan on getting on stage to sing tonight?"

Even in the dim room Sierra noticed the tip of the older man's ears color with embarrassment. "I've never tried. I'm not sure I have the nerve."

Gram placed a hand on his arm. "You sing in the shower, don't you?" He nodded after a moment. "There you go. This is less embarrassing because you will be fully dressed."

Sierra covered her mouth and looked away from the stunned look on the elderly gentleman's face. Was Nix regretting sitting down?

"Sierra. What was this drink called again?"

Her gaze swung back around to witness her grandmother polishing off the drink she held. "Gram. You may want to slow down a tad on those."

"Posh." She waved a hand in her direction. "Clara and I have a designated driver."

Nix rose from his seat. "What are you drinking and I'll buy this next round."

Gram winked and rose and threaded her arm through his. "Such the gentleman. I'll go with you." She glanced at Clara. "You want another one?"

Clara shook her head and gazed after her friend as they walked away. A smile tugged at her lips. "It's good to see Cora having some fun." She sighed. "I've worried about her."

Both looked on as the couple stopped at the bar and waited to get the bartender's attention. "Gramps left a huge hole in her life." She met Clara's gaze. "I'm glad you are doing things together."

A faraway look stole over her features. "I lost my Ernie some time ago. It gets easier, but I remember how hard it is at first."

"Is that why Gram has made it her personal mission to find me a man? She's looking for a project to keep her entertained?"

"Mostly." She shrugged as a gleam entered her eyes. "You'd like my grandson."

"He was the intended target of last night's escapade, wasn't he?"

A guilty look eased across her face before she took another sip of her drink and looked away.

Alarm bells clanged in her head. She looked about at the crowd. What were the two up to tonight? "Clara? What does Gram have up her sleeve?"

The DJ chose that moment to start the Karaoke back up again. "Okay. Break time is over. Our next participant is Tracy. Let's all give her a hand."

Sierra's head began to pound as one singer after another poured their heart and soul into the words crossing the screen in front of them. How long did Gram and Clara plan on enduring this evening? She glanced at her companions. They sang along with the man crooning on the stage. Nix sat silently in between them with a serene smile upon his face.

In front of each of them sat several empty glasses. She frowned at how much alcohol they'd consumed. As the next singer took the stage, her grandmother groaned.

"Not her again." She staggered a bit as she eased off her seat. "My drink is empty. I need another one."

Sierra rose and placed a restraining hand upon her arm. "Gram. Are you about ready to call it an evening?"

A finger wagged in her direction. "Are you being a fuddy duddy again?"

She wasn't going to rise to the bait this time. "No.

I'm speaking with the voice of experience."

"Maybe Sierra's right, Cora." Clara was a little steadier than her compadre, but just barely.

Her words slurred as she exclaimed, "It's not over until the fat lady sings." She glanced at the stage and started laughing. "Oops. Too late. The fat lady is singing."

Sierra gasped in horror as her grandmother's rude words reverberated around them.

"What did you say?" The growled question came from a beefy bald guy a couple of tables away. *Uh-oh. Now you've done it, Gram.*

Cora didn't back down as the man rose.

Sierra scooted in between the two. "Now listen." Her hand hit a solid wall of flesh as he approached. *Oh geez.* "Gram, please tell the nice young man you're sorry and didn't mean what you said."

The brute crossed his arms across his chest. "Yes. Gram." His words were uttered with a sneer. "I want you to apologize to my wife."

She squinted with laser focus as she swayed a little. A hand rose to rub her temple. "Where are my manners? You were right, Sierra. Those drinks pack a punch." She skirted around her and patted the man's beefy arm and cringed. "Geez. You're built."

It was Sierra's turn to growl. "Gram."

"All right. All right. Keep your shirt on." She straightened to her full height of five-foot seven-inches and firmly stated, "I apologize, young man. My comments were rude and uncalled for. I'm sorry."

"I should have known you'd be behind this disturbance."

Fingers of dread crawled down Sierra's spine. Her

chin dropped to her chest as she recognized the male voice.

"Hi, Sheriff. We've kissed and made up. There's no reason to haul us in."

Oh, Gram. Would you please zip it. She finally turned to face the man standing a few feet away. Gone was the nervous father of a couple of hours ago. In his place stood the long arm of the law. "Sheriff." She cast a glance at the injured party in this fiasco. "Like Gram said, everything is smoothed over."

The sheriff's gaze bounced from her grandmother to the man standing nearby. "Is that correct, Stan?"

Beefy dude stared hard into Gram's unflinching gaze before he uncrossed his arms and shrugged. "Yeah. We're good."

The sheriff nodded. His gaze didn't quite meet hers. "I suggest you take your party home, Ms. Scott. Before anyone gets hurt."

Chapter Ten

Sierra flipped to her side and stretched. Lazing about could become habit forming. A contented sigh left her lips. She blinked and a scream tore from her mouth. Gram hovered over her by the side of the bed. Adrenalin and blood pressure were in a tight race on doing her in. "Gram." She scooted up against the headboard. "Are you trying to kill me?"

"You know…" she squinted and leaned in a little closer. "When was the last time you waxed your eyebrows?"

Unbelievable.

"If you don't close your mouth, a fly might find its way inside."

Irritation began to stomp out the alarm buzzing through her system. "Get out." She pointed a finger at the open bedroom door. Hadn't she locked it before she went to bed?

A nonchalant wave addressed her demand. "I wanted to see if you were all right. Do you have a hangover? It's after eight o'clock." She crossed her arms over her chest.

It was obvious Gram had no lasting effects from the previous night's drinking expedition. If her peppy attitude was anything to go by. "No. I'm not hung over. Are you?"

"Of course not. Why would I be?"

Why indeed? "You know a simple knock on my door would have worked." The bedspread hung halfway off the bed, and she slid out from under it. "By the way, I'm on vacation. Do I need to remind you of that fact? I deserve to sleep in." She shooed her with her hand. "Go, Gram." She cast a glare over her shoulder before entering the bathroom. "I'm going to take a shower. Alone."

Steam rose from the stall as she pulled her sleep shirt over her head. Her thoughts turned to the previous evening as she stepped under the stream of water. The image of Cade's stern disappointment crept into her mind. Any type of connection she'd assumed she had with him the previous afternoon was surely crushed. Disappointment bubbled below the surface. The first real interest she'd shown in a man and the events of the evening most likely had him running for the hills.

A few moments later she toweled her hair and left the bathroom. The clock on the dresser read a little before nine o'clock. No wonder Gram had checked on her. The whole lurking by the bed had creeped her out. She was surprised she hadn't caught her with a mirror under her nose to see if she was still breathing.

The kitchen was quiet as she entered. A glance about proved she was the only occupant. Propped up against the coffee pot was a note. She picked it up and read the brief missive. *Join Clara, Georgette, and me out in the apple orchard behind the house when you are awake and civil.*

Civil? "I'll show you civilized…" she muttered before wadding up the note. *Who's Georgette?* She searched through the cabinets for a thermos. She had a feeling this morning was going to be more than a one coffee cup type of day.

As she exited the house she breathed in a deep breath. There was a nip of autumn in the air. Muted giggles echoed from behind the house. She followed the sound of merriment and found herself on a path leading to a small grove of apple trees. Gram and Clara stood beside a ladder with matching wide brimmed hats upon their heads. A big basket sat on the ground. "Don't either of you think about climbing one rung." Each wore a guilty expression as she joined them.

"We were waiting." Gram smiled and gave her a quick hug. "Are you awake now?"

"Gram." She leaned back from her embrace and shook her head. "We need to work on your manners."

Her eyes twinkled. "I'm afraid it's too late for me."

The funny thing is she had a point. "You're telling me. Good morning, Clara." Seconds later something cold and wet touched her leg and the second scream of the day wrenched from her lips. She jumped and almost fell as she turned to confront whatever threat was imminent.

"Sierra. Don't scare Georgette." Gram reached down to pluck a miniature black and white potbellied pig from the ground. A squeal rent the air.

With a hand upon her chest, she took a steadying breath. The comedy of errors from this vacation kept escalating. The pig gave a quiet grunt and smacked its lips.

"Do you want to hold her?"

Call her crazy, but she did. She extended her hands and carefully took Georgette into her arms. She cradled the miniature pig and grinned down at her. Was she smiling back at her? She tickled each ear before scratching under her chin. "Aren't you a sweetie?" She gave Clara a quick look. "How long have you had her?"

"She's about six months old. My neighbor gave her to me."

Gram shared a wink with her. "Clive has a crush on Clara."

"Oh phooey. Go on."

But if Sierra wasn't mistaken, a blush stained her cheeks. "Well. I guess if we're going to get any apples picked today, I'm going to have to put you down." An answering grunt made her smile before she placed the pig on the ground. She waddled away with a smack of her lips and wiggle of her curly tail. "Now." She placed her hands on her hips. "Tell me what you need me to do."

Less than an hour later the basket was full. She stepped from the ladder and wiped her hands down the legs of her jeans. The sweet smell of apples filtered toward her nose. "Are you making more apple butter, Clara?"

She ambled forward and shook her head. "No. Some will be used in the bob for apples booth and the rest will be pies for the church auction."

"Speaking of pies. Am I too early to grab a piece?"

A young fair-haired man crossed the yard and gave Clara a hug. This must be her grandson. The intended victim of their matchmaking.

"Travis." She returned his hug. "I didn't know you were coming for a visit."

His gaze collided with hers over his grandmother's shoulder and his lips curved into a smile. "I can't stay too long." He leaned back to indicate his uniform. "I'm out this way on official business."

A concerned expression filtered across Clara's face.

"I hope it isn't anything serious."

"Nothing life threatening. I'm heading to Clive's place. He's volunteering to help with security this weekend. He doesn't have any use for those new-fangled computers, so we couldn't email instructions to him." He offered his hand to Sierra. "I don't believe we've met."

Very smooth. "Sierra Scott." She smiled and extended a hand.

"Oh, pooh. Where are my manners? This is my friend Cora Scott and her granddaughter. They're visiting and helping me get ready for the apple festival."

Merriment crept into his gaze. "I hear you got a proper welcome to the community the other night. I'm sorry I missed it."

She felt a wave of warmth climb into her cheeks.

Clara flicked him on the arm. "You behave yourself, young man."

A deep chuckle rumbled in his chest. "But you and I both know misbehaving is more fun."

"Do you have time for a cup of coffee?"

He placed a kiss on his grandmother's cheek. "Not this time." He leaned down to pick up the heavy apple basket. "I need to be on my way. I'll place this in the kitchen." His laughing blue eyes collided with her gaze. "Nice meeting you, Sierra. I hope to see you this weekend. Save me a dance."

She shook her head as he strode from the yard. Charismatic little bugger. If she hadn't met the sheriff first, would she have felt an attraction toward Travis? Nearby someone cleared their throat. Her gaze met Gram's. "Yes?"

A smile rose to her lips. "Nice looking young man, isn't he?"

71

Her gaze swung between her grandmother and the other conniving senior citizen. Their Cheshire cat grins identical on their faces. "You're both incorrigible." She clucked her tongue and bent to pick up Georgette. She cradled the little pig close and whispered in her ear, "Want to help me call the office, sweetie?" With a step backwards toward the house she fished her cell from her back pocket. "I'll be back to help make pies."

Chapter Eleven

The sweet aroma of apples, cinnamon, and nutmeg lingered in the Jeep's cab. Sierra waved good-bye to the church ladies before each disappeared inside the church. The morning's activities yielded five pies for the auction. Gram and Clara were taking an early afternoon siesta while she delivered the baked goods. She only had one more stop. The basket with the left-over apples for the bobbing booth also resided in her vehicle. She shook her head at the cagey way her grandmother delivered the news the apples needed to be delivered to the sheriff's department. Was this another attempt to throw her together with Travis? If nothing the pair was tenacious.

She made a right-hand turn and noticed the station about halfway up the block. Several parking spots were available in front of the red brick building, and she slid into one. Nervous anticipation made her stomach flutter at the thought of seeing Cade again.

The building had an automatic door and she pushed the button with her elbow as she wrestled with the basket.

A middle-aged woman looked up from the front desk and rose. "Can I help you?"

"I hope so. Clara Lakewood asked me to deliver these apples." She shifted the container to a better position on her hip. "They are for your booth at the festival."

"Oh yes. We were expecting them. Follow me and we will put the goodies in the conference room."

Sierra trailed behind the clerk and placed her load on the table.

"By the way, I'm Wendy Toft." She offered a hand.

"Nice to meet you, Wendy." She released her hand and asked, "What are your responsibilities at the station?"

"A whole bunch of this and that. I'm dispatch, receptionist, file clerk, and whatever else needs done around here."

"Don't forget to tell her we would be lost without your help."

Her pulse leapt as she turned to observe Cade leaning against the door jamb. She studied his features looking for any clues on his disposition. "Good afternoon, Sheriff."

His lips quirked and he straightened. "What do you have for us in here?" He leaned in to study the container's contents.

The peal of a phone echoing from the front desk had Wendy scurrying from the room. "Excuse me."

Seconds ticked by in silence. He cleared his throat. "I want to thank you again for helping Riley shop yesterday. I haven't seen her this pleased with a purchase in ages."

"I had fun." She leaned against the table next to him. Her gaze met his. "You should be proud of your daughter. She's a nice young lady."

He chuckled and quipped, "She was on her best behavior." His gaze shifted and seemed unfocused for a moment. "The last few days have hammered home the fact she's not a child anymore."

She brushed her shoulder against his. "Boys tend to drive that detail home quicker than anything."

"You're telling me."

His nearness was causing havoc on her senses. She leaned away from him. "I…"

"About…."

Their words collided as they both spoke. He chuckled and shook his head. "Go ahead. Ladies first."

Her mind went blank. What words had he interrupted? She couldn't remember what she meant to say. "Oh no. I insist. You can go first."

He paused as if searching for the right thing to say. "I need to talk to you about last night."

She'd known this was coming. "I know." Was he going to tell her goodbye?

"You realize you dodged a bullet last night at Walt's bar, don't you?"

She bit her bottom lip and ducked her head in a nod. "Yes. Gram…" What could she say? "I went as the designated driver and chaperone for Cora and Clara."

"And things got out of hand?"

A groan escaped and her gaze met his. "You think?" She rose and paced a few feet away. "I've thought about this a lot this morning. I wouldn't put it past my senior citizen companions if their whole plan was to cause the ruckus on purpose."

"But why?"

She turned back around to face him and shrugged. "My guess. To get you or Travis to come out on the call."

Disbelief and shock reflected in his eyes. "Your grandmother is worse than a dog chewing on a bone."

"Don't I know it."

A thoughtful look passed over his features. "I say

we give Cora what she wants."

She frowned as she attempted to understand where this conversation was headed. "A bone?"

His lips quirked up in a lopsided grin. "Close, but not quite." He unfurled his body from its lounging position against the table and crossed the small space separating them. "My schedule is going to be crazy this weekend with the apple festival's activities, but not so frenzied that I couldn't spend some time with you. Maybe grab some lunch."

She smiled as her nerves began doing a happy dance. "I'd like that."

"Sheriff."

Sierra jumped at the interruption.

Wendy smiled and apologized. "Sorry. I hate to disturb you, but the mayor is waiting at his office. His meeting ended early, and he wants to go over this weekend's activities."

"Thanks, Wendy." His brown gaze met hers. "I'll see you later?"

Sierra left the station giddy with the prospect of spending time with Cade over the weekend. The earlier fear that he would hold last night's trouble against her fizzled into oblivion. As she clicked her key fob to unlock the Jeep, her cell rang. She removed her phone from her back pocket and glanced at the caller ID. Mark. Oh no. She took a calming breath, hoping there wasn't a crisis at the office. "Good afternoon."

"Sierra. Do you have a moment? I hope I'm not interrupting anything."

"Not at all. I'm out running a few errands." *Please don't tell me I need to come back to the office to handle an emergency.* She cradled her phone to her ear with her shoulder and climbed into the Jeep.

"There are a few matters needing your attention and I will email those to you this afternoon." He cleared his throat. "But there is another issue I need to discuss with you in regard to Mr. Dunham."

Michael? She recalled the awkward conversation she had the day before. "Is there a problem?" She eased back in the driver's seat and gazed out the side window.

He made another attempt at clearing his throat.

Goodness. She'd never heard him for a loss of words. "Mark. Lay it out for me. What seems to be the trouble?"

"I had a meeting set with Mr. Dunham this morning and he didn't show up."

She frowned and leaned her head back against the headrest. "Were you able to get ahold of him to reschedule?"

"No."

Frustration with the attorney settled in her stomach and she began tapping her fingers on the steering wheel. "Was this meeting the one to discuss the final paperwork for the expansion?"

"Yes." He inhaled deeply and rushed on, "I just got off the phone with the managing partner at Gates, Carey, and Bell. Mr. Dunham didn't show up for work this morning and they haven't heard from him."

She rubbed her forehead. "Do I need to come back to the office?"

"No. Everything is under control."

Uncertainty rattled around in her mind. "Are you sure?"

"Positive." He cleared his throat. "One other thing." He paused. "I consider you a friend. Not just my employer."

Sweat beaded her brow and the palms of her hands. She closed her eyes and took a calming breath. "Mark. You've been an anchor for me over the last couple of years. If I've done something…"

He interrupted her midsentence. "Oh no. It's not you. It's another matter involving Mr. Dunham."

She suppressed a groan as it threatened to climb up her throat. "Has Gram been coaching you on what to say about me dating our legal counsel?"

A nervous chuckle echoed over the receiver. "Cora has a way of letting her wishes be known, but no. Mr. Dunham came by my office yesterday afternoon and became anxious when he didn't know where you were."

Where was their attorney's angst coming from? "I spoke with him late yesterday afternoon."

"Did you tell him where you were?"

It wasn't a national secret, but she hadn't. "No. I told him if he had any matters to discuss he could call you." She put down the window to create a breeze inside the Jeep's cab. "Why?"

"He tried pumping me for your location and when you would be back."

What was so urgent? She frowned. Why did he need to know where she was and when she planned on returning. "Does he have some legal documents only I can sign?"

"No. Everything is in order. There are a few documents, but I can sign those. There is no need for you to cut your vacation short. Everything else can wait until you are back in town."

"Well. It sounds like you have everything under control. Except, of course, for our rogue legal counsel."

His chuckle echoed in her ear. "I didn't want to bother you with this, but I thought you should know. Try to enjoy the rest of your vacation."

"Thanks, Mark. I will."

Chapter Twelve

The feeling of excitement she'd experienced moments before as she'd left Cade's office was depleted. Sierra didn't understand Michael's behavior. She couldn't understand his possessiveness he'd displayed the last couple of days. Yesterday he'd accused her of blowing off her responsibilities and then turned around and did it himself when he didn't meet with Mark this morning.

An unexpected gust of wind blew her hair into her eyes. She glanced out the window and noticed dark clouds had crept in while she was on the phone. Gone was the pleasant afternoon sun. A shiver skittered down her arms. She shook her head and tried to re-summon the anticipation for the upcoming weekend. Thoughts turned to Cade's request to spend time with her. She smiled as she forced negative thoughts about Michael from her mind. What she needed was retail therapy. If she was going to the festivities, she needed an outfit and knew exactly where to go. The Sunshine Boutique was getting to be her favorite place in town.

As she entered the store a girlish squeal tore through the air. "Sierra." Riley sat behind the counter next to the cash register with an open textbook in front of her.

"Hi, Riley." She tilted her head. "Do you work here after school?"

She shrugged her shoulders. "Kind of. Most days I

ride the bus home, but today I'm helping Nanny out. She's at the bank." She stood and made her way around the counter. "Can I help you with something?"

"Well, it's been brought to my attention there is a dance this weekend. I don't think I packed anything appropriate. I'm here for my own retail therapy today."

"Fire."

She frowned as she tried to translate what fire meant. "Is that a good thing?"

Riley rolled her eyes. "I forgot you and Dad are old. It means amazing."

Up to this point she had never considered herself old, but at this moment Riley made her feel all of her thirty-two years.

"Riley. I've taught you better. You don't talk to my customers in that manner." An older woman stood inside the store's entry and paused before she made her way behind the counter to stow her purse.

A sheepish expression stole over her face. "Sorry, Nanny. Sierra. I didn't mean anything by it."

A chuckle bubbled in her chest. The exchange reminded her of some of the chats with Gram lately. Conversations change over the ages, but truly they don't. "I think I'll take my aging self over to the dress rack and browse."

Riley giggled but smothered it with a hand when her grandmother frowned at her. "Um. I need to study. I'll see you tomorrow, Sierra."

She slid a few hangers aside and pondered each selection before moving to the next item.

"Do you need any help?"

Startled, she jumped.

"I'm sorry. I didn't mean to scare you."

Sierra laughed and shrugged her shoulders. "I guess I was deeper in thought than I realized."

"I'm Mary King by the way."

She accepted the offered hand and smiled. "Nice to meet you, Mary."

"How do you know Riley?"

"We go way back." She smiled and chuckled. "To yesterday afternoon. I helped her shop."

"Oh. You're Cade's friend. Riley modeled her outfit last night when she was at my house." She leaned in and whispered, "Thank you so much. Cade was pleased and truthfully so was I. Teenage girls are hard sometimes."

"If I'm honest..." She glanced over at Riley to see if she paid attention to their conversation. "I haven't had much interaction with teenage girls."

Mary waved a hand in dismissal. "Nothing's changed since you were younger, I'm sure."

Had she been a normal example of a teenager? She'd always been a hard worker, disciplined and focused on working her way to taking over Scott Enterprises from her grandfather. "What does one wear to the apple festival, Mary? You know. Someone my age."

They both shared a laugh before she turned to another rack. "I think you can't go wrong with something along these lines."

Sierra studied the brown dress. The mid-length sleeves were made of lace with a scalloped neck. She took the dress from Mary and turned to the nearby mirror. The handkerchief hem fell about mid-calf. It was flirty and fun.

"I like it."

She turned and laughed at Riley's endorsement. "Thank you for your approval."

"Try it on."

Her gaze met Mary's. "I guess my fairy teen godmother has spoken." A few minutes later she exited the dressing room to three sets of eyes focused on her. When had Cade joined them? A wave of shyness overtook her as his gaze roamed over her frame. Did his gaze hold more sparkle than normal? "What do you think?"

"You need boots."

His lips tipped up in a grin at his daughter's declaration.

She glanced down to study the squirrels dancing on her socks. "And maybe some socks. These are kind of wild." Her gaze met his. "I guess I'll be dumping some cash at the boot store."

"It's only fair. Since I spent some of my hard-earned money there yesterday." He rested an elbow on a nearby clothes rack. "I'm off duty. Care if I tag along?"

A stunned silence and two sets of shocked gazes darted between her and Cade. Riley recovered first. "I can eat at Nanny's. You could take Sierra to dinner afterwards." She directed a wink in her dad's direction.

Sierra tried not to laugh, but a small snort escaped. She shrugged and stated, "A girl has to eat."

Less than an hour later Cade and Sierra were led to a booth at a place called the Beef Joint. She could feel the curious gazes of the locals as they followed their progress to their table. It was obvious the citizens of Harts Valley weren't used to seeing their sheriff out with a woman. The knowledge gave her a warm fuzzy feeling. "Tell me, Cade. You bring all your women here?" His gaze swung from hers to the curious onlookers. From a few tables over an older couple waved. She smothered a grin as he didn't reply and took a seat.

An awkward silence ensued until the waiter broke it moments later. "Good evening." He handed each a menu. "Tonight's special is the prime rib. If you haven't had it before I would definitely recommend trying."

Once their orders were given, he leaned back and took a sip of his tea. "Any shenanigans from your senior partners in crime I need to know about this evening?" He waved a hand in the air. "You know…in case I need to add extra security at the festival."

The firm gaze resting on her almost made her squirm. "I can't guarantee a problem free weekend, Sheriff. After all, it is my grandmother we are talking about."

A sparkle appeared in his eyes. "She has kept me on my toes over the last few days."

"I had my doubts when Karaoke was suggested." She fiddled with the end of her napkin. "But I had a fun time until…the incident."

He leaned forward and whispered, "Maybe I can join you next time."

Laughter bubbled in her chest. "You mean without the nine one one call?"

"Exactly." He shook his head. "But you wouldn't extend the offer if you heard me sing."

"What?" She put her hand on her chest. "You don't croon like Michael Bublé?"

"Melissa always said it's a good thing I was nice on the eyes because I couldn't sing worth crap."

She had to agree with Melissa's assessment. Would it be too intrusive if she asked what happened to his wife? She leaned across the table and touched his hand. "If I'm not being too forward. How did she die?"

"It's okay." He covered her hand with his own. "She was killed in a car accident, but the underlying problem was a brain aneurism."

The sadness in his eyes made her hurt for him and Riley. "I'm sorry." The words seemed paltry considering the loss he'd suffered.

His gaze landed on their hands and he began to caress hers with his thumb. "Thank you."

Tingles of awareness traveled up her arm. She shook off the sensation and retrieved her hand from his grasp as their food arrived. The first taste was all the waiter had promised and then some. "Oh wow. This is delicious."

After a few bites of his own meal, he tilted his head and studied her for a moment. "You're on vacation. Have you ever told me what you do for a living? I think we got interrupted the other day when I asked."

She put her fork down and squirmed under his curious gaze. The last few days she'd been incognito, with not a worry about who she was or what her portfolio contained. "I own a business in Tulsa."

His eyebrow quirked. "What type?"

She waved a hand. "I took over my grandfather's tech company when he passed."

"Computers?"

"Yes…and more." She shrugged her shoulders.

He studied her silently for a moment. "Are you involved in something illegal?"

"What?" She almost choked as a ripple of shock traveled through her. "No."

"Then why do I get the feeling you don't want to talk about what you do for a living?" His eyes narrowed. "Your details are sketchy."

"Sorry." She wiped her mouth with her napkin and

turned her gaze away from his for a moment. "It's when I start talking about my company, I get certain reactions and I don't want to get the same response from you." Her gaze swung back to connect with his as she took a deep breath. "My grandfather was Charles Scott." She waited for the name to register.

A frown wrinkled his brow for a split second before a look of surprise and recognition crossed his features. "As in Scott Enterprises?"

"And there it is." She pointed an accusing finger at him. "Don't you dare start treating me any different than you have up to this point." The twinkle entering his eyes made her wonder what he was thinking. Laughter rumbled up his chest and burst from his mouth. "What?"

He leaned forward, his elbows resting on the table. "How much money could I get from selling my naked story to the tabloids? I have a teenage daughter to raise."

Heat rose to her cheeks at his nearness and the slight suggestive tone in his voice. "Oh. I don't know." She shrugged. "I hear exclusives pay well."

The evening held a chill as they left the restaurant later. She hated to see the night end. A parking lot light blinked a couple of times before staying on. The keys rattled in her hands as she pushed the unlock button on her key fob. "Thank you, Cade. I enjoyed the meal and the company."

"If you haven't noticed the stares I received tonight, I don't date much." A light chuckle escaped his lips. "Okay. Not at all. But I enjoyed the evening as well." He did a quick perusal of the parking lot before he took a step closer. "Your gallant knight hasn't received compensation for all the rescuing he's been doing lately."

"Oh. What is the going rate for rescues?" She covered her mouth and bit her lip to keep from smiling. "Do you take credit cards?"

A low growl rumbled from his chest. "Wrong type of compensation. I was hoping for more of a personal touch."

Anticipation strummed through her body as she took a step closer toward his warmth. "I think we may be able to negotiate terms we can both agree upon."

His fingers caressed her cheek briefly before he leaned in and captured her upturned lips with his own.

Her lids fluttered closed as her thoughts scattered. The touch was gentle, explorative, and all too soon…gone.

"I've been wanting to kiss you since I first saw you."

She inhaled a calming breath and tried to control her racing heart. "Oh, really?" The imp in her made her ask, "You mean when you found me naked? Your first thought was kiss this woman?"

His chest rumbled as he chuckled. "Okay. That may not be my first thought." He stroked her lower lip with the pad of his thumb. "But a close second."

Several emotions washed over her, desire, excitement, and lastly fear. She liked him. Really liked him.

"I'll see you tomorrow at the festival." He brushed a piece of her hair behind her ear. "Good night, Sierra."

"Tomorrow." The huskiness of her voice surprised her. "Night, Cade."

Chapter Thirteen

A blast of cooler air skirted around her body as she stepped from her Jeep. A shiver shook her frame. Autumn was upon them. The jacket she'd brought on this expedition wasn't enough. Maybe Gram would have an extra one to wear which provided a little extra warmth.

A shadow crossing the yard caused her to pause as she retrieved her shopping bags from the back seat. What wild animal was lurking out of the reach of the lighted house? Her tense muscles relaxed as the distinctive sound of a grunt carried in the night. "Georgette? Is that you?" The little pig shuffled closer. Worry sprang up inside her mind. "What are you doing out here so late? Did momma Clara forget to put you in bed?" She shifted her bags to her left hand and leaned down to pick up Georgette. A shiver shook her little body and she snuggled her close.

When she entered the house Gram was in the sitting room working on her crochet project while Clara stared at the television set.

"Look who I found roaming around."

Clara gasped and rose from her seat. "I was so worried about her." She wrestled the wiggling pig out of her hands. "I couldn't find her when I went outside to put her in the shed."

"It's getting colder outside. I'm sure she'll be happy to go to bed now." Sierra smiled as Clara walked from the room chastising Georgette.

"You missed dinner." Gram placed her project down in her lap. "Clara put the leftovers in the refrigerator if you are hungry."

"That's okay. I ate while I was in town."

Her sly gaze slid over to catch her own. "By yourself?"

"Actually." She eased out of her jacket. "No."

"Oh. Anyone I know?"

It was hard to dismiss the flicker of satisfaction appearing in her eyes. "Go ahead. Pat yourself on the back."

She picked up her crochet needle and wrapped her finger with thread. "I don't know what you're talking about."

"Yes, you do, you ol' meddler."

A shrewd look crossed her features. "Since you've met Travis, you like him, don't you?"

It seems she didn't know all after all. "Gram. I ate with Cade."

"Oh." Her fingers paused on her task a moment before starting up again. "Did you now? Interesting."

Why didn't she believe she was as clueless as she let on? "I have the feeling you already knew that anyway?" She picked up the packages she'd placed on the floor. "I have some emails I need to catch up on. What time do I need to be ready for the festival tomorrow?"

"Clara opens her booth at eight in the morning."

"I'll be ready." She started down the hallway. "Night, Gram."

She hung her dress and placed her new boots in the wardrobe. A yawn threatened, but she placed her laptop on the bed. A glance at her inbox indicated she had the expected email from Mark. She looked it over briefly. He did seem to have everything under control at the office. She snapped her laptop lid shut. Tomorrow vacation mode continues.

****

The porch swing rocked back and forth as Sierra cradled a cup of coffee in one hand and petted Georgette with the other. She glanced down at her companion. After she woke, she went in search of the little pig. If she didn't know better the critter snored in contentment.

As the sun rose, a colorful display stretched across the sky. When was the last time she enjoyed watching a new day begin? If Gram hadn't coerced her out of the office, she wouldn't be here basking in the moment.

She gently repositioned Georgette onto the bench seat beside her before pulling up a knee to rest her chin on it. Life and work balance plagued her thoughts this morning. Thus, the reason she sat watching the sunrise.

"What a serious look you're wearing."

She tilted her head to study her grandmother standing by the swing. "I'm contemplating life's decisions. It's a thought-provoking moment. But I'm not sure I should be doing it on my first cup of coffee."

"Care to share?"

"My thoughts? Coffee? Or my seat?"

"All of the above." She chuckled and waved a hand to indicate the small pig. "But I see you already have a swing buddy."

"Come on, sleeping beauty." Sierra drained the last of her coffee, set the cup aside, and lifted a heavy-eyed Georgette onto her lap. "Let's give Gram some space."

Cora gave the pig a quick pet. "So. Are you going to tell me what's troubling you?"

"Was Gramps happy?" She put the swing in motion with a push of her foot. "Did he ever feel he was missing out on life because of the business?"

A thoughtful look crossed her features as she contemplated her questions. "I know he had regrets. But the company was one of his passions." She chuckled and winked. "Well, besides me that is."

"Of course. Definitely a given." Her laughter mingled with her grandmother's.

She looped an arm around her shoulders. "I know I strong-armed you into coming on this vacation. But I've been worried about you. There's more to life than work."

"I know." She leaned her head against Gram's. "The last few days have made me realize what I've missed."

"Such as?"

"What I've learned?" She raised her hand and counted off on her fingers. "You're never too old to skinny dip. Don't trust relatives with your car keys." She leaned up to shoot what she hoped was a knowing look at her. "And keep your eyes open for love."

"My, you've had a busy week."

She patted her hand. "Thank you for reminding me to take the time to stop and smell the flowers."

****

The fairgrounds bustled with activity as she followed Clara's car into the parking lot. Unlike the other day, everywhere Sierra looked people milled about. A small area was sectioned off with carnival rides. It wouldn't be long before lines would be forming where the games were set up. She smiled in anticipation. Maybe she would find the time to try her hand at winning a stuffed animal.

The sun peeked through a small amount of billowing

clouds that drifted overhead as she crossed the parking lot. The late-night storm that blew through in the middle of the night was nowhere in evidence. Gram and Clara were already at the booth when she caught up with them. "What can I do to help?"

Clara placed a cash box on the table and started to uncover her merchandise. "I think everything is under control. Do you want to roam around to see what the other booths have to offer?"

"You don't have to ask me twice. Call if you need my help." The next thirty minutes she wandered from one vendor to the next. She'd found gifts for her mom, dad, and sister. The goat soap on the table in front of her had several pleasant fragrances. She held up another bar labeled lavender and decided her assistant would like the scent. Her gaze snagged on one labeled "rustic man." After a small sniff, she realized the vendor had captured Cade within the bar. *Maybe this is the soap he uses*. Was it strange she was going to buy a bar as a reminder of him? Before she could change her mind, she paid for both.

"Hi, Sierra." Riley bounded to an abrupt stop next to her.

"Good morning. You're up and about early."

"Dad dragged me out of bed because he had to be here before all the vendors started showing up this morning." A dramatic sigh left her body. "I'm on my way to find some coffee for him. Want to come with me?"

A quiver of excitement fluttered in her belly. The brief kiss from the evening before replayed in her mind. She'd known he'd be busy today with the festival, but Riley had given her a reason to see him earlier than expected. "Sure. Let me check first with Gram and Clara to see if they want anything."

Several customers were gathered around the booth as they arrived. "Looks like you ladies are doing a brisk business. Do you need my help?"

Clara waved aside her offer. "We've got a handle on things."

"Who's this?" Gram smiled at Riley as she handed change to a customer.

"This young lady is Riley Collins." Sierra smiled at the teen. "This is my grandmother Cora Scott."

"Hello."

"Oh, you're the sheriff's daughter?"

"Yes, ma'am."

"Ma'am?" She laughed and glanced at Sierra. "Do I detect a slight Texas drawl?"

Riley shrugged her shoulders. "I probably picked it up from Dad."

"Riley and I are going to get some coffee. Do you and Clara want a cup?"

"No, dear. Clara brought a thermos and we are sharing. Go on. Have fun."

"I need to stop at my Jeep." She held up her purchases. "I don't want to carry these around all day."

As they made their way across the fairgrounds Riley glanced at her and asked, "Did you and dad have fun last night?"

She peeked sideways at her. Had she been okay with her going out with Cade last night? The suggestion had come from Riley. But how did she really feel? "You didn't mind me going to dinner with your dad, did you?"

Riley stopped walking and met her gaze. "No. Of course not. I worry about him."

"Why?" The statement was more mature than what a fifteen-year-old would make.

Her gaze shifted and she started walking again. "He hasn't dated anyone since my mom died." She stopped to join the line for coffee at the concession trailer. "He likes you. I can tell."

"Are you okay with him liking me?" Sierra couldn't read her expression.

She stopped chewing on her bottom lip and smiled. "Yes. I hope he doesn't blow it."

Or she doesn't. The evening before he hadn't seemed to object to her being Charles Scott's granddaughter, but maybe he hid it well. Suddenly she got jostled as Riley scooted into her from behind. "Riley?" What was she doing?

She tried to duck behind her shoulder. "It's Noah."

"Really? Which one?" A few feet away there were several young men standing and talking in a group.

She leaned in and whispered, "The one in the navy-blue T-shirt."

The young man in question was tall with dark hair peeking from under the brim of a black cowboy hat. He smiled at his friend and Sierra could understand Riley's crush. She frowned as she contemplated how to get her to connect with Noah.

"Miss?"

"Oh." She turned to collect the coffee being offered. "Thank you." She turned with the cup in her hand. "Do you want me to deliver this to your dad so you can hang out with Noah?"

Her mouth opened and closed before she shook her head. "What do I talk about?"

"Maybe something along the lines of good morning

for starters."

"But."

She prodded her forward with a hand to her back. "Ask him if he would be interested in playing some of the games? Or hanging out."

Her boot heels dug into the gravel as she pushed. "But he's with his friends."

"No pain, no gain."

Confusion clouded her gaze. "What?"

"Go on." Once again, she nudged the teenager. "Try it."

She straightened before taking a tentative step forward, but took a quick glance back at her, as she got closer to the cluster of boys.

Sierra made a shooing motion with her free hand. Noah's gaze rested on Riley a moment before he said something to his friends and broke away to step toward her. She watched as he said something to Riley and her shyness melted away. Moments later they strode away toward the carnival games and rides. Cade was in for another panic attack. She removed her cell from her purse and sent a text to him.

—*I have a coffee for you. Where are you?*—

—*I wondered where my barista was with my order. I'm at the front gate.*—

—*Your brew is on the way.*—

A few feet away from her destination she paused to admire Cade as he sat upon the back of a big black horse, his gaze intent on the crowd. Riley wasn't the only one crushing on a cowboy. "One black coffee."

He turned in the saddle, smiled down at her, and reached for the Styrofoam cup. "Morning."

The horse shifted and studied her with big blue eyes.

She placed a tentative hand on his nose and caressed it. "Hello big guy. How are you this morning?"

"He was getting testy because he didn't have his java." He took a sip and frowned. "Where is Riley by the way?"

"Did you take your blood pressure medicine this morning?"

"Uh-oh." His gaze scanned the crowd again. "Noah?"

"Yes." She tried to disguise the smile threatening at his distress. "I'm glad she finally divulged his name. They were heading toward the games when I left them."

He appeared deep in thought before he asked, "What did you think of him?"

She chuckled and shook her head. "If I was fifteen…I'd be crushing on him."

"Wonderful." A low growl discharged from his lips.

She placed a reassuring hand on his thigh. But instantly regretted the action as an electric current traveled through her fingers to her unsteady heartbeat. What was the point she was going to make? Her gaze met his. "I should let you get back to work."

He tipped the brim of his hat and smiled. "I expect you to save a couple of dances for me tonight."

"I'll see what I can do, Sheriff."

Chapter Fourteen

Cade watched as Sierra strode away. Today she had her shoulder length hair fashioned in a braid. He recalled how his gut took a punch the previous evening when she'd appeared from the dressing room in the dress she now wore. She'd taken his breath away. The invitation to dinner Riley suggested surprised him. But he was glad she'd recommended it, or he might have chickened out on asking for himself.

The knowledge that Sierra was Charles Scott's granddaughter still stunned him. The news should have bothered him. What would a woman like her see in a man like him? But he silently argued, she's a lot more than a successful businesswoman. She was a vivacious woman and he realized he had it bad. He shook his head and struggled to put his mind back on the job at hand.

"Sheriff."

Travis guided his mount alongside him and pointed to his coffee cup. "I wish I had a lovely woman delivering my coffee." His gaze followed her as she retreated and blended into the growing crowd. "I didn't have a chance, did I?"

His gaze met Travis' and he took another sip of coffee before answering. "I'd like to think this relationship may go somewhere, but I'm not sure how this is going to play out."

"Think positive, Sheriff." He turned his horse and

headed off in the opposite direction. "I'm going to check on how Clive is doing at the South gate."

****

Was the purple teddy bear mocking her? Sierra renewed her effort to shoot the water gun at the center of the target. She could have bought the damn bear times two as much cash as she'd shelled out already. But it was the principle of the matter.

"I wouldn't quit your day job."

The husky male voice whispering in her ear made her finger slip on the trigger. "Hey. Stop it." The final bell rang, and she hadn't won her prize yet again. "Look what you did." She turned her gaze to meet Cade's twinkling gaze. "Are you taking a break?"

"Yes." He sat down on the neighboring stool. "Are you free for lunch?"

"Maybe." She gazed back at the stuffed animals and tilted her head toward the prize. "How's your aim? I'll accept your offer if you win that bear for me."

"The purple one?" He pulled out his wallet and counted out some bills. Less than five minutes later he took the bear from the attendant.

Accepting the prize, she smiled at him. "Thank you."

"You're welcome." He helped her to her feet and steered her toward the food trailers.

The warmth of his hand on her back sent a tingling thrill through her system. "What fine dining experience are you offering a girl?"

He chuckled and pointed to the row of concession trailers. "The options are limitless."

"Hmm." She studied a nearby menu. "Are the loaded nachos good?"

"Remember the meal we had at Betsy's Café the other day?"

"Her stand?" The thought produced a loud growl from her stomach. She rubbed her belly. "I think my stomach endorsed the nachos."

"The platter is enormous. Want to share an order?"

She grinned and hugged the bear to her chest. "Why, Sheriff, are you worried about your figure?"

"Not necessarily. You'll thank me. Trust me."

Moments later they sat at a picnic table with a heaping plate sitting between them. She shook her head in wonder. "I think they forgot to pitch in the kitchen sink."

He chuckled and handed her a napkin. "I hate to say I told you so, but…" He spread his hand to indicate the platter.

Flavor burst upon her tongue as she took the first bite. The jalapenos added just enough spice. "I'm going to gain twenty pounds on this trip." A wave of warmth filled her cheeks as his intent gaze studied her. And she was sure it wasn't from the jalapeno's heat.

"I'll watch your figure for you."

This was what her life was missing. She needed more of this. More of this man. "Why, Cade, are you flirting with me?"

A small frown furrowed his brow. "I'm a little out of practice, but that's what I was trying to achieve."

She took a chip, and cheese trailed behind as she took a bite. He picked up a napkin and wiped her chin. The gesture caught her further off guard. "I think you're doing fine." She captured his hand before he could drag it away and interlaced her fingers with his. An electric current ran up her arm as he gently caressed her hand with his thumb.

"Dad?"

The deep hue rising on his cheeks proved he was embarrassed to be caught by his daughter in an intimate moment. The mood was shattered, but he recovered quickly. Sierra tried to pull her hand from his grasp, but he held firm.

He finally glanced at Riley. "Hi, honey."

A knowing grin graced her lips. "Having fun?" Her look encompassed both her and Cade.

With her free hand Sierra pointed toward the bear sitting next to her on the bench. "Look what your dad won for me."

"Way to go, Dad." She leaned in and whispered, "Noah will be here in a minute. I want you to meet him. Be nice. Please, Dad."

He feigned innocence as he pointed to his chest. "Who, me? Why would you think I wouldn't be nice?"

The byplay between the two proved the love and closeness they had for one another. She shifted and doubt wormed its way into her thoughts. Was she fooling herself into thinking she could have a close bond with Cade? Riley?

"Mr. Collins." Riley's young man had joined them as Sierra's thoughts had wandered. "I'm Noah Spencer."

Cade released her hand and stood to shake the young man's offered hand. "Nice to meet you, Noah."

Sierra observed Cade as he tried to make the meeting less intimidating.

"You too, sir."

He indicated the huge plate of nachos. "Are you guys hungry? We have plenty. We could share."

"Thanks, Dad, but we're grabbing a hamburger with

friends."

A forlorn look crossed his features briefly before he disguised it. "I'll catch up with you later then."

"Okay. See ya, Dad." Riley smiled at her. "Have fun, Sierra."

A long sigh left his lips as they walked away. She placed a hand on his arm. "Are you okay?"

"The truth?" His brown gaze caught hers. "No."

It was hard to imagine what he was going through. His little girl was maturing before his eyes. Her thoughts scattered as an incoming message pinged on her cell. She frowned at the message displayed. It was from Mark.

—I still haven't been able to get in touch with Mr. Dunham. I've contacted the managing partner at Gates, Carey, and Bell and I plan to meet him at their office this afternoon. I will let you know when the paperwork I was supposed to sign yesterday for the expansion is finalized.—

"Something wrong?"

"Hmmm." Her gaze swung back to connect with his. "It's my chief financial officer Mark Simons. He's meeting with the attorney this afternoon to sign some paperwork."

He shook his head. "Why does that make you frown?"

"Oh. Was I?" She leaned forward. "Remember me telling you about our attorney, Michael Dunham?"

"Yeah. He's the one your grandmother doesn't want you to date."

"Right." Her chuckle eased the concern bubbling up in her chest. "Anyway. When I talked to Mark yesterday, he said Michael missed an appointment to sign the final documents for our expansion project."

"Has he said why he missed the appointment?"

"That's just it. Mark hasn't been able to reach him. He's made an appointment this afternoon with one of the managing partners at the law firm we deal with to sign the paperwork."

"On a Saturday?"

She shrugged her shoulders. "What can I say? We are a big account for them."

"Do you need to go back to Tulsa for the meeting?"

"No." She shook her head with determination. "Mark has everything under control."

"Whew. For a moment I thought I was losing my opportunity to slow dance with you this evening."

"Not a chance, Sheriff. Your name is written on my dance card."

He sat back down and grasped her hands. "In pencil or ink?"

She gave his hands a squeeze. "Non-erasable ink."

"The best kind."

"You know. I had a serious discussion with Gram this morning."

"Oh." He tilted his head. "What about?"

"Me. After being off the last few days I realized how I've been running constantly since my grandfather passed." Her gaze met his. "I've deceived myself into thinking I was happy with how my life is going. But I've decided I deserve balance in my life."

He was silent a moment before he asked, "In this balancing act…is there room for someone special?"

Her heart skipped a beat. Was she ready to take this leap? "Maybe. Are you putting in your application?"

He smiled and gave her a wink. "I'll work on my resume."

His words caused her stomach to surge with hope. "I'd like that."

He leaned forward and captured her lips in a swift kiss. "But speaking of work."

"I know." Her lips tingled from his brief caress. "Lunch break is over."

"I need to get back to protecting and serving." He gave her hands a final squeeze and rose.

She picked up her bear and purse. "I'll see you tonight, cowboy. I'm looking forward to those promised dances."

He tipped his hat. "Yes, ma'am. So am I."

Chapter Fifteen

As he strode away, he cast a look over his shoulder and winked. A laugh bubbled from her lips as she hugged the bear. The flutter in her stomach indicated the relationship was worth pursuing.

Snippets of the conversation with Gram from the morning played in her head. If she was going to do more with her life than eat, sleep, and drink work, she needed to make changes. And soon.

Shifting the stuffed animal to her other arm, she lifted her cell and placed a call to Mark.

"Sierra. For someone who is supposed to be on vacation, I seem to hear from you often."

She chuckled before apologizing. "Sorry, Mark. What comes with time on your hands when on vacation? Soul searching. And I've done some of that the last couple of days."

"Understandable."

"What time are you going to the attorney's office this afternoon?"

"I'm meeting Mr. Gates at two o'clock. Please tell me you aren't cutting your visit short to come to the meeting."

His groan made her chuckle. "That is the farthest thing from my mind." She strolled a few paces and shook her head. "No. I have some other matters to discuss with you. Do you have a moment?"

"This conversation sounds serious. But now is the opportune moment. Kelly's out with the kids picking up pizza."

A sigh escaped as she made her way back to the picnic table she just vacated and sat. "First. I take it you still haven't been able to contact Mr. Dunham."

"Correct. I've tried multiple times. Since the paperwork is time sensitive, I contacted Mr. Gates this morning and he was happy to meet with me to go over the documents."

The disappearing act worried her a little. Had something happened to the attorney? "Am I the only one who finds it strange that Michael is ghosting you?"

"No. My gut is telling me something is off. Another reason I chose to call Mr. Gates this morning."

She tried to force down the unease settling in her stomach. "Let me know what you find out."

"I'm sensing there was another reason for your call."

A chuckle escaped. "You know me too well. I had a discussion with Gram this morning and I want to post a position for a Chief Information Officer." She inhaled a huge breath before she admitted, "I need help. I can't keep up with the pace I've set over the last couple of years."

There was a moment of silence before he replied, "Thank goodness. This is the best news I've had all day. I'd hoped this vacation would knock some sense into you."

"Well, it has. When I'm back in the office I would like your help outlining the position." A heavy load lifted from her shoulders as she disconnected the call less than fifteen minutes later. The sigh escaping her lips was one of relief. The wheels were in motion.

Her phone rang instantly. Did Mark forget something? She smiled as she read the ID. "Hi, Emily. Are you calling to check to see if Gram has done me in?"

"No." A laugh echoed from the speaker. "I'm actually calling to see where you are?"

She frowned at the question. "Are you suffering from memory loss? I'm in Harts Valley with Gram. Didn't we have this discussion a couple of days ago?"

"No, silly. I know you're in Harts Valley. So am I."

An excited squeal burst from her lips. "Awesome, Em. It's been forever since I've seen you."

"I know, right? I figured if my high-powered sister can take a few days off, well so can I."

"Oh wow. Did you let Gram know you were coming?"

"Are you kidding me?" She snorted and chuckled. "That would give her time to make plans for me."

"If she suggests going swimming…run."

Her laughter floated over the receiver. "Noted. Are you going to tell me what direction to point my car? Or is this a scavenger hunt?"

A bubble of laughter escaped. "Sorry. I got caught up in the fact you were joining us. I'm at the fairgrounds."

"Just a sec." An irritated curse reverberated through her speaker. "My GPS says less than five minutes."

"Great." She gave her bear an excited squeeze. "I'll meet you in a bit." Eagerness spurred her to walk a little faster. She'd last seen Em a couple of months ago and for only a brief moment. As she strode into the parking lot, she caught sight of her sister's sedan easing into a parking space. She shouted as she eased from her car, "Hurry up. You're missing all the fun."

She turned and shrieked before she hurried over for a hug. "I've missed you."

"Right back at ya."

Emily leaned back and studied her a moment. "Look at you. I love the dress, boots, and bear. Vacation looks good on you."

"Thank you. I needed the break more than I realized. Mind if Mr. Bear makes himself comfortable in your car while we go see the sights?"

"Since when have you got good enough at playing games to win a prize?"

"Hey." She punched her in the arm. "I have game."

A snort left her lips as she rolled her eyes. "Since when?"

"Okay." She shrugged her shoulders before she gave the animal a final hug. "I may have had some help."

A watchful look crossed her face as she stopped mid-stride. "Please tell me you aren't here with that attorney Gram's told me about."

"No." She shot what she hoped was a dirty look at her sister. "Doesn't anyone believe I can pick a suitable man to date?"

She shrugged and threaded her arm through hers. "It's just you're out of practice."

There was some truth to the statement, but it still stung. Why did everyone think she was helpless in the romance department? She shook her head. "Never mind. What do you want to do first? Have you eaten?"

She held up a hand. "Slow down. I don't know and no, I haven't."

"We have so much to catch up on, but let's get you some food." She led her toward the line of concession trailers. "How did you get off work on such a short notice?"

"I asked." She shrugged her shoulders. "It's funny how asking works in the real world."

"You're funny." They stopped to examine one of the white board menus.

"Mmm. I haven't had a Philly steak sandwich in ages."

"You order and I will snag a picnic table." A few feet away a family vacated a table and Sierra sat down. It was fun to watch the people milling about. Everyone seemed to be enjoying the warmth from the sun. The autumn day couldn't have turned out nicer.

"What else have you done this week?" The aroma of fried onions and peppers wafted toward her from Emily's tray as she sat down.

"Gram and Clara locked my keys in my Jeep." She swiped a fry from her plate. "I retaliated by not acknowledging their antics. I think it drove them crazy."

"What else?"

"What do you mean?"

She swallowed and wiped her mouth with a napkin. "Have you seen the officer who rescued you?"

"The sheriff?" She swiped another fry. "Actually, I had dinner with him last night and lunch with him today."

"Ah." She tilted her head and smiled. "He won the bear?" The sandwich lay abandoned as she asked, "You like him? Tell me about him."

Is it just like? "His name is Cade Collins, and he has a fifteen-year-old daughter, Riley."

"Divorced?"

"No." She frowned and shook her head. "His wife passed away a few years ago."

"Hi, Sierra."

A few feet away Travis sat atop a horse. He grinned down at them as he leaned on the saddle horn. "Well. Hello, Deputy. Are you just now taking a lunch break?"

"You know Cade." He tipped the brim of his hat upward. "Such a task master."

She chuckled and indicated a spot at the table. "Do you want to join us?"

"Sure." He gathered the reins in one hand and dismounted. "I never turn down a meal with a couple of beautiful ladies."

She smiled as he grinned and gave her a wink. "Flatterer."

"Buck deserves a scoop of oats." He turned to lead his horse away. "I'll be right back."

"Who was that?"

Emily's gaze followed the cowboy's retreat. "Are you checking out his buns?"

A red hue rose in her cheeks. "Maybe."

Laughter bubbled in her chest and burst from her lips as her sister fanned herself. "That's Clara's grandson Travis. The man Gram and Clara have tried to set me up with over the last few days."

"Either you're crazy…" She shook her head. "Or blind."

Her words rattled around in her mind as her thoughts turned to Cade. "Neither, actually."

"Ladies." Travis swung a leg over the bench seat and sat. "Thank you for saving me a seat."

"No problem. Have you been by your grandmother's booth?"

He shook his head. "No time. Is she doing well?"

"She was busy when I stopped by this morning." His

gaze left hers and traveled to Emily. "Travis, did you know I have a sister?"

He popped a french fry into his mouth. "Don't believe so."

"Travis Lakewood." Her hand fluttered toward her sister. "Meet Emily Scott."

He wiped his hands on a napkin and reached out to clasp her hand. "Nice to meet you."

"Likewise."

Sierra hid a smile behind a hand as Travis continued to study her sister. The charisma he'd shown the other day didn't seem to be in attendance.

Travis was the first to break the silence as his gaze swung to her. "What's this I hear about Karaoke?"

"Man." A sigh escaped. "You'd think you men gossip worse than women do."

He shrugged his shoulders. "What else are we supposed to talk about? Cade was catching me up on the calls I missed the other evening."

Emily's gaze bounced from her to him. "Catch me up. You sang Karaoke?"

She shrugged and a snort escaped. "Sort of. Gram and Clara did most of the belting of tunes."

A frown formed in between Emily's eyes. "Really?"

"Aretha Franklin. They had liquor encouragement." She laughed as her sister groaned and cradled her bowed head in her hands. "That's not the worst of it. Gram almost got into a bar fight and arrested."

Emily's gaze swung back to Travis'.

He put down his sandwich and held his hands up in self-defense. "Not me. I wasn't on duty the evening in question."

"You know." An expectant gleam entered her eyes.

"I took next week off from work. Do they have Karaoke weekly?"

"Next Wednesday." He lowered the sandwich again without taking a bite. "If you'd like I could pick you up."

"I'd enjoy going with you."

He turned to include her. "Maybe you could convince Cade to come along as well."

"I have it on good authority he can't sing worth crap." She laughed at the look of astonishment on his face. "Cade's words, not mine."

His lips quirked upward. "Finally, something Cade doesn't do well."

Sierra sat quietly as the next few minutes Emily and Travis bantered back and forth on their favorite country artists. Maybe Gram and Clara's matchmaking would come to fruition after all.

The sandwich in front of Travis disappeared and he rose. "I hate to eat and run, but I need to make sure everything is going smoothly." He tipped his cowboy hat to both of them. "Thank you for your company." He turned to walk away but turned back. "Emily? You going to the dance tonight?"

"Oh. I didn't know there was one."

Sierra nodded and caught her sister's gaze. "She'll be there."

"Great." He smiled and offered a small wave. "I'll see you ladies later."

Emily placed her elbow on the table and rested her chin on her hand. "He's nice."

She fluttered a hand in front of her sister's face. "Let's go find Gram. She'll be happy to see you." She chuckled and shook her head. "And to hear you like Clara's grandson."

Chapter Sixteen

"Gram. Look who I found." Sierra smiled as Gram gasped and skirted around the table to hug Emily.

"I didn't know you were coming."

"I know." She shared a knowing look with Sierra. "It's better that way."

"Don't get cheeky with me, young lady." She turned toward Clara. "This is my granddaughter, Emily. This is my friend Clara Lakewood. I don't believe you've met."

"Hi, Emily. It's nice to meet you." She finished making change for a sale and turned back to ask, "Do you have a place to stay? I have an available room at the house."

"Thank you, Clara. I had hoped to share a room with Sierra."

She waved aside her intent. "Nonsense. I have an extra room. When Cora said she was coming with guests, I made sure all of the bedrooms were ready." She patted Emily's arm. "So, the arrangements are settled."

Sierra examined the number of jars on the booth's table. "Wow. You almost sold out."

Clara beamed, excitement evident in her expression. "It's been a great day." She consulted her watch. "I'm packing up everything in about thirty minutes."

"Oh." She looked around at the other vendors. "Emily, do you want to see what the other booths offer before they close down for the day?" She threaded her arm through her sister's. "There are several with homemade jewelry. You can add to your collection."

They roamed from booth to booth until the vendors began to pack up. The sweet smell of caramel drifted to her nose. When was the last time she had a caramel apple? "Em, do you want a caramel apple?"

"Is that what I smell? I'd love one. It's been forever since I've had one."

She joined the line and smiled at her sister. "Was your work unhappy with you when you asked for a few days off?"

She shrugged her shoulders. "Not really. The next couple of weeks will be slow."

"I made a decision today."

They moved up in line before Emily asked, "Oh. About what?"

"I'm going to slow down. I've talked to Mark Simons about hiring someone to assist me."

Her mouth gaped as she stammered, "Wow. I didn't see that coming."

She shrugged and fluttered her hands. "You weren't the only one who stated their concern this week about my health."

"Have you told Mom and Dad?"

"Not yet."

Emily pulled her in for a quick hug. "They are going to be thrilled."

She turned to order two apples. "My treat."

"Thanks."

Juice dribbled down her chin at the first bite. She laughed as she caught the trickle and wiped the caramel off her upper lip with a napkin. "I've forgotten how messy these things can get."

Emily joined in her laughter as she battled with her own messy bite. "You're not the only one who will be wearing it."

Her gaze caught on a man standing a few feet away observing her as she made another swipe with her napkin at her chin. The laughter bubbling from her lips stalled. She blinked and lowered her apple. On her tiptoes she strained to locate the man again in the meandering crowd. Surely, she'd imagined seeing Michael Dunham and the glint of malice thrown in her direction.

"Sierra. What's up?" Emily turned to look in the direction in which she gazed.

The sticky caramel was left forgotten on her lips. What was Michael Dunham doing in Harts Valley? Or were her eyes playing tricks on her? "I thought I saw the company's attorney, Michael Dunham, in the crowd."

Her sister's gaze bounced from one person to the next in the throng of nearby people. "Really? Why would he be here?"

She shook her head. "I don't know."

"It was probably someone who looks like him." Emily put her arm through one of hers. "Come on. Let's finish these apples and go check out some of the games."

****

Cade swung down from the saddle and grabbed the reins. A few feet away his neighbors, the Millers, waved.

"Good evening, Sheriff."

"Clyde. Martha. It's a nice night, isn't it?" He shifted his feet. "You going to the dance?"

Clyde put his arm around his wife's waist. "Wouldn't miss it."

"I'll probably see you over there. I need to get my horse settled for the evening." After bidding the older couple good night he led his horse into the barn. The day had gone smoothly, but the evening hours of the festival were usually the ones that caused him stress. The sun was setting, and the alcohol flow always picked up at this time.

He soaked in the peace and quiet of the barn as he unsaddled his horse. The smell of fresh hay wafted to his nose and the only sound to interrupt the silence was Ace munching on the feed in his stall. As he combed and stroked his horse's coat thoughts of Sierra eased in and chased away the worry the evening may hold.

He relived the brief kisses they'd shared since the evening before. The tempo of his heart picked up. A sigh escaped as he reminded himself to proceed with caution. Sierra was a very wealthy woman. Her confession the previous evening had caused him pause. The business she owned was a multimillion-dollar company. Why would she be interested in a local sheriff with a teenage daughter? Was he chasing rainbows?

Tulsa wasn't far away. Could they continue a relationship once her vacation ended?

"Cade. You still in here?"

He gave Ace a final pat on his hindquarter before he exited the stall. "Down here, Travis."

Travis rounded the corner with his mount trailing behind. "Clive stopped me to let me know he's taking a thirty-minute break."

"That's fine." He pulled his cell from his pocket and checked the time. "I'll text everyone to meet outside the community center for a brief security meeting at seven."

"Everything okay?" Concern washed over his features.

Cade noticed the frown marring his deputy's brow.

N. Jade Gray

How could he explain the unease he was feeling if he didn't understand it himself? "Just making sure we have all the t's crossed and the i's dotted."

He turned to lead his horse into the neighboring stall. "Did you know Sierra had a sister?"

"No." He frowned as he realized he didn't know her all that well.

Travis stuck his head back out from the pen. "Her name is Emily. I'm hoping to catch a dance or two with her tonight."

"She's in town?"

"Yes. Drove in this afternoon to surprise Sierra."

It seemed like a lot had happened since he'd lunched with Sierra. "Can I gather from the gleam in your eye you're interested in furthering her acquaintance?"

Travis finished taking care of his horse and exited the stall. "I wouldn't be opposed. Maybe we can all go together to Walt's bar next week to sing Karaoke." Travis laughed at Cade's groan. "Heard you can't carry a tune."

"That's putting it mildly." He slapped him on the shoulder. "Let's go meet the others."

Chapter Seventeen

"Yoo-hoo. Ms. Scott, wait up."

Sierra turned to see the waitress from the other day rushing toward her. What was her name again? She tried to recall as the other woman sidled up next to her and Emily.

She huffed and puffed for a moment before a huge smile broke across her face. "Remember me? My name is Betsy. You were eating at my café with the sheriff the other day." She took a much-needed breath before continuing. "Remember? I told you I thought you looked familiar." She waved a magazine in her direction. "As soon as I saw a copy of this month's edition of *Business Women* I remembered where I've seen you before. How long are you in town?"

She opened her mouth to reply, but Betsy rushed on.

"I'm the president of the local business association and if you could come speak at our meeting next week, I would appreciate it."

She waited a second to see if the woman would interrupt her reply. "What day is your meeting and the time?"

"We meet next Thursday at six pm. I tweeted this morning that I planned on asking you to speak at our meeting. The response I've received on Twitter is phenomenal. Can you do it?"

The woman was like a steamroller. She could see

why her business was so successful. Persistence was a virtue in her case.

A deep chuckle sounded to her left. "Betsy. Do you have an off switch?"

Embarrassment made Betsy's cheeks turn bright red. "Sorry. The sheriff's right. I do tend to ramble when I get excited about something."

Sierra's gaze met Cade's and she shared a smile with him. "It's okay, Cade. I don't mind speaking at Betsy's meeting."

He shrugged his shoulders with indifference before he leaned in to whisper in her ear, "Don't say I didn't warn you."

Tingles spread down her spine at his nearness. His breath caressed her ear a moment before he pulled away. "Um." She swallowed and tore her gaze away. "Betsy, get with me in a couple of days to discuss specifics." She bumped into Emily as she shifted from one foot to the other. Goodness, she'd forgotten her sister was standing nearby. "Oh. Where are my manners?" Emily's eyes twinkled with amusement at her awkwardness. A serious razzing was bound to happen as soon as Cade took his leave. "This is my sister Emily."

"Sheriff Cade Collins, ma'am." He brushed a finger to the tip of his cowboy hat. "It's nice to meet you."

"You too, Sheriff. I've heard so much about you."

His brow quirked in silent question before his gaze met hers. "Anything worth repeating?"

A chuckle escaped her sister's lips. "Maybe." She started backing up toward the building behind them. "I'm going to find Gram. See you inside."

Warmth spread up her neck. She was sure a blush resided in her cheeks. They grew warmer as he laughed.

"Why, Ms. Scott, if I didn't know better your cheeks are redder than the first time we met."

Betsy cuffed the sheriff on his arm and came to her aid. "You leave her be. I don't want her leaving town before my next meeting because of your teasing."

"Sheriff." Travis strode up and interrupted their banter. "Everyone is assembled. We're waiting on your instructions."

Cade tipped his hat and smiled. "Ladies. If you will excuse me. Duty calls." He turned to go but glanced back over his shoulder. "Don't forget you owe me a dance, Ms. Scott."

Sierra watched him walk away and caught herself wanting to fan herself. How had she become smitten so quickly?

"Ms. Scott?"

Betsy still stood beside her with a bemused expression upon her features. "It's good to see the sheriff happy." She patted her hand. "I'll be in touch about next week's meeting."

As Betsy strode away an eerie sense of being watched stole over her. A scan of the crowd roaming about didn't produce the cause of her wariness. She rolled her shoulders as she tried to dislodge the sensation. Loud laughter from a nearby carnival ride made her jump. What was wrong with her?

She took a tentative step toward the community center before she cast one last glance about. Upon crossing the threshold, the sound of a fiddle brought her gaze to where the band warmed up on a makeshift stage against the far wall of the building. Chairs were arranged along the outer walls. She smiled as a memory of one of her high school dances filled her mind. Boys had awkwardly lined one side of the gym and the girls the other.

Cade and his officers were gathered by a side entrance across the room. His attention was fully focused on the instructions he relayed.

"I see you can't seem to tear your gaze away from him."

She rolled her eyes before her gaze met Emily's. Before she could reply she continued.

"I totally don't blame you. I can see why you are fascinated." She tilted her head and indicated with a nod in the other direction. "Who's with Gram?"

Over by the punch bowl their grandmother stood with an elderly cowboy. Her laugh rang across the room. Sierra smiled at the youthful look upon her face. "The gentleman's name is Butch Nix. She met him the other evening at Karaoke."

"She looks happy."

"She's not the only one." She pointed to an animated Clara. "I think he might be her neighbor who has the hots for her."

Emily made a pouty face and sighed. "Is it sad my grandmother and her friend get more male attention than I do?"

Across the room it looked like Cade was dismissing his officers and Travis started in their direction. She shot a sly look at her sister. "You can quit practicing your oh woe's me act. Opportunity is approaching."

"Hey, ladies." Travis stopped and gave them a quick smile. "The band is about to start playing." His gaze landed on Emily. "Before my duties take me away can I fit in a dance?"

Sierra smiled as they walked away toward the dance

floor.

"Care to join me? We can't let them have all the fun."

Butterflies flittered about in her stomach as she turned and met Cade's gaze. "Why, Sheriff, how can a girl refuse?"

"She can't." He held out his hand and she placed hers inside the warmth of his grasp.

As they started to two-step across the floor, she marveled at the oneness she felt. Never had she seemed so graceful with any other partner. Even when he twirled her, she didn't falter. It's true. Even the most awkward individual can dance with the right person. Her gaze met his and her smile froze. Here was a man who didn't care who she was related to or what assets she held in her name. The music faded into the background as he lowered his head. Her lips sizzled as he softly caressed them.

"Sheriff. Is there a reason you are making a public display of yourself with my granddaughter?"

Sierra broke the kiss and tried to muffle the snort of laughter in the collar of his shirt. Her cheek vibrated as his own chuckle rumbled in his chest.

"After you get through canoodling, we've saved a table over in the corner. Join us."

"Canoodling?" His brow rose in confusion.

She snickered at his bewilderment. "What? You've never canoodled, Texas?"

"I probably have, but I didn't realize there was a word for it."

She stepped back but kept an arm around his waist. "Come on. Don't think Gram won't hunt us down."

The table's chatter ceased as they arrived. Curious

eyes zeroed in on them. "What?"

A giggle escaped Emily's lips. "For someone who doesn't like to be on public display, you hit it out of the ballpark." She pointed toward a lady standing nearby.

Cade groaned and announced, "I'll be right back."

"Who's that?" Puzzlement clouded her mind.

"She's a busy body." Clara shook her head. "But her official title is photographer for our local paper."

"Oh boy." The happy bubble from moments before burst. "Does she know who I am?"

"I saw her talking to Betsy." Clara nodded with affirmation. "She does."

Cade rejoined the group after a brief conversation with the photographer. "Monica has promised not to publish the photo."

She nibbled her lip. "Do you believe her?"

"Verdict is still out." His gaze bounced from hers to the woman still staring at them from a short distance away.

Should she care if the tabloids get ahold of the photo? She cast a sideways glance at Cade. She wasn't sure how this relationship would blossom, but it wasn't something she wanted to hide. "I don't care."

Again, silence permeated around the table. Gram was the first to break the hush. "Good for you." She rose and turned to Butch. "Come on, cowboy. I think it's time for a dance."

As one by one the occupants of the table deserted them, she cast a glance at the man standing silently beside her. "Do you have time for another spin around the floor?"

The frown furrowing his brow cleared. "As fast as everyone disappeared, I was beginning to wonder if my deodorant failed."

She took his hand and slipped into his arms as a slow song began to play. A candid whiff of his neck proved this cowboy still smelled as yummy as he had this morning. "I have no complaints, Sheriff."

His lips quirked upward. "You're the one who matters."

The song seemed to end way too soon. As he eased away from her arms, she missed the warmth of his embrace immediately. "Time to get back to work?"

"Sorry. As much as I enjoy holding you in my arms, I need to check to see if there are any problems." He tilted her chin and brushed a kiss across her lips. "Don't go falling for another cowboy in my absence."

"Then you better hurry back, Sheriff." His chuckle trailed behind him as he crossed the floor and headed for the exit.

Realizing she stood in the middle of the room with couples two-stepping around her, she angled back toward the table where Gram sat alone.

"It's good to see you so happy." She motioned for her to take an adjacent seat. "I've worried about you lately."

The highhandedness her grandmother had taken to get her to take a vacation still irritated, but if she hadn't left the office, she wouldn't have met Cade. "Gram. Are you expecting a thank you?"

With a tilt of her head, she nodded. "Yes, I am."

"Thank you for your intervention." She leaned forward and wrapped an arm around her shoulders in a brief hug. "I realize now how much I needed a break."

"See. It pays to listen to your elders."

"Careful. Your ego is showing." The couples on the

dance floor drew her attention for a moment.

"Out with it?" Gram's gaze snagged her own. "What's bothering you? The sheriff?"

A chuckle bubbled in her chest as she shook her head. "Were you a mind reader in another lifetime?"

"No. I know things because I've made a few laps around the block." She placed a hand on her knee. "What's your concern?"

The events from the last few days replayed in Sierra's mind. "Am I setting myself up for heartache?"

"What do you mean, dear?"

She nibbled on her bottom lip and shrugged. "We're so different."

"Meaning what? You have more money than he does?"

She shook her head. "No. Cade is a single dad with a teenage daughter. Is there even room in the equation for me?"

"Only if you let it."

Her phone vibrated in her pocket and her thoughts scattered when she pulled her cell out. Three missed calls and two texts from Mark. She frowned and scooted her chair out and rose. "Excuse me, Gram."

"What's wrong?"

"Nothing, I hope." She took a few steps backward. "But I need to call Mark back."

Gram's brow knotted with concern. "I hope there aren't any problems at the office."

"We'll see. I'm going to step outside. It's too noisy in here to hear a phone conversation." She stepped through the exit and shivered at the noticeable drop in temperature. A quick rub up and down her arm didn't dispel the chill. In her other hand her phone vibrated.

Then again. And again. She glanced at the metal building she'd exited. It must have blocked the signal. Every single missed call and text were from Mark. Had something gone wrong at the attorney's office? A foreboding feeling shimmied down her spine. This wasn't good.

Without bothering to listen to the voicemails or read the texts she redialed Mark's number. He answered on the first ring. "Mark? Is something wrong?"

"Sierra…"

A gasp escaped as her phone was ripped from her hands. She spun around and anger replaced her surprise. "Mr. Dunham? Michael? What the hell do you think you're doing?" He extended his arm and held the phone out of her reach. She could hear Mark asking if she was there and swore again when Michael purposely disconnected the call.

"Tsk. Tsk. Such vulgar language, Ms. Scott."

When she leaned forward again, he jabbed something hard into her ribs. A wince escaped and she glanced down to see he held a small pistol. She wrestled down the panic rising in her mind. "What are you doing?"

He tossed her phone aside and it skidded across the paved sidewalk. The sound of glass cracking permeated the night. He grabbed her arm and dragged her toward a blue four-door sedan. Both the passenger and driver's door were wide open.

She dug her boot heels into the gravel, and he yanked harder on her arm. The small cross body purse draped across her stomach spilled its contents as he continued to pull and drag her toward the car.

"Sierra? Are you okay?"

Michael turned and pressed the pistol harder against her side for a few seconds before pointing it at Riley. "Listen, little girl. Don't come any closer."

Sierra wheezed in horror. Her gaze collided with Riley's. "Please, Michael. I'll go with you, just don't hurt her."

Shock registered in the younger girl's eyes before they began to tear up. "Sierra?"

Michael wrenched her sideways and produced a zip tie. "Riley. Please. I'll be fine. Go find your d…" She cast a quick glance at her captor. Did he know she was Cade's daughter? How long had he observed her today? The pinch of the plastic tightening on her wrists made her flinch. As he turned her toward his sedan she balked.

"Get in."

She glanced over her shoulder at Riley. "Find the sheriff."

None too gently he pushed her forward. The tip of her boot caught on the gravel, and she almost fell. He grasped her upper arm and helped her into the front seat. The door slammed and he skirted around the front of the vehicle.

He paused before sliding in and yelled a command at Riley. "Tell the sheriff no FBI. I'll be in touch." The overhead dome light cast an eerie shadow upon his face as he shut the door. "Don't try anything funny."

Chapter Eighteen

The bright lights and noises from the arcade games were ten times brighter and louder than the music in the community building. Cade's stride quickened. The sooner he made his rounds, the quicker Sierra would be back in his arms.

As he weaved through the crowd, a shout echoed from a few feet away. He broke into a jog as he rounded one of the food trailers. Two middle-aged men yelled at each other, and punches began to fly. What would an apple festival be without a show of a flex of muscle? The hint of alcohol permeated from both. "Hey." He leaned in to take one by the scruff as Travis ran up from the opposite direction to take the other in hand. "Police. Break it up."

"It's nuthin', officer."

The slurred words produced another whiff of alcohol. Cade's eyes watered at the potency. "What seems to be the problem?"

Travis wrestled with his young man a moment as he tried to get free. "He came over and started wailing on me." His accusing finger pointed at Cade's captive. "I didn't do nothing to him."

His gaze met the man's blurry gaze. "Is this true? Why did you start hitting him?"

A hiccup escaped. "For money."

He frowned at his words. "You tried to rob him?"

"Nope." He swayed a little as he continued, "Had to earn my hundred dollars."

Cade's stomach lurched as he tried to get the man's attention. "Someone paid you to start a fight?"

Hiccup. "Yup."

He exchanged a glance with Travis before asking, "Do you know the person who paid you?"

"Nope."

He gritted his teeth at the man's blasé attitude and obvious drunken stupor. The irritation strumming through his body ratcheted up a notch. "Was it a man or a woman who paid you?"

"It was a dude."

Finally, they were getting somewhere. "Are you able to point him out to us?"

He took a step and stumbled as he peered at the gathering crowd. "Not here."

Anxiety grew as he tried to understand what was going on. His gaze scanned the throng of people as well. No one stood out as the culprit. Was this man a victim of a prank? "Travis. Cuff him."

"Hey." He yanked his arms as he tried to free himself. "Whatz the charge?"

"We'll start with public intoxication and disturbing the peace." He exchanged a glance with his deputy. "Do you have this under control?"

Travis unclipped his cuffs from his belt and nodded. "I'll take him down to the station." After securing the intoxicated man into a nearby patrol car, he shouted back toward Cade, "I'll be back shortly."

"Dad."

The near scream tore down his spine. Riley rushed toward him with tears clinging to her cheeks. "Damn."

He raced over and grasped her shoulders and studied her face. "What's wrong?"

A sob tore from her throat as she tried to wipe the wetness from her face. "Sierra."

"What about her?" Fear crept up his spine.

She struggled a moment with words before she blurted, "He had a gun."

The bottom of his stomach fell as dread filled his being. The other shoe just dropped. Whoever had paid their inebriated participant had showed his hand. His grip tightened on her arms and immediately loosened his hold when she gasped. "I'm sorry, honey. Tell me what happened."

"I went looking for Sierra." A hiccup escaped. "Cora told me she'd stepped outside to return a phone call." She inhaled a deep calming breath. "When I found her there was a man dragging her toward a car." With difficulty she swallowed. "He had a gun shoved in Sierra's side. And then…" A fresh set of tears formed. "He aimed the gun at me."

For a few seconds he closed his eyes and tried to focus. Now wasn't the time to let his fears run amuck. He had a job to do. Opening his eyes, he peered into hers and gently prodded, "Is there any other information you recall? Think. This is important."

"He said to tell you no FBI." She held out her palm. A cell with a shattered screen was upon it. "This is Sierra's phone."

Thoughts whirled in his mind. This wasn't a random crime. He took the smashed phone and was surprised to see the screen light up before requesting a code to unlock it. "Do you remember anything else?"

She nibbled on her lip and was deep in thought for a

moment. "She called him Michael."

"What?" His thoughts spun to the conversation they had at lunch. Wasn't Michael the name of the attorney Sierra mentioned? The one working with Scott Enterprises?

Riley nodded with determination. "Yes. I'm sure she called the man Michael."

"That's good, darling. Can you tell me where she was taken from?"

"The car was parked outside the exit in the back of the building."

Elation skittered up his spine. There was a security camera in the vicinity. He needed to examine the footage. "Can you describe the vehicle?"

"It was a dark blue four door." A frown furrowed her brow. "I believe it was a Ford."

He gave her arms an encouraging squeeze before drawing her in to enfold her in a big bear hug. An uncontrollable shiver shook his frame. His baby was safe, but some kind of mad man had taken Sierra. Leaning away from the embrace, his gaze met her anxious one. He wiped a tear from her cheek with the pad of his thumb. "I need you to find your Nanny and stay with her."

"But Dad." She started to shake her head. "I want to help."

"No." The exclamation tore from his mouth. "I don't want to worry about you, too." He leaned his chin on top of her head. "Promise me you will do as I say." The sound of running footsteps reached his ears.

"Riley, are you okay?" An out of breath Noah raced up to them and skidded to a stop.

"Can you help Riley find her grandmother? I have

some police business to take care of."

"I'll make sure she's all right." He put an arm around her shoulders. "You can count on me, sir."

"Thank you, Noah." Once they were safely back inside the community building, his mind scrambled in five different directions. His jaw tightened as he tamped down the anger rising inside of him. It was time to focus on the job he needed to do. Not lose control.

Chapter Nineteen

The silence in the cab was suffocating. Sierra's mind scrambled back to Michael's demand not to involve the FBI. It seems her vacation got derailed into a kidnapping. *Please let Cade find me quickly.*

Gravel flew as Michael punched the gas as he rounded a corner. Did she dare confront him as he drove? The streetlights became fewer and fewer as they left the town's city limits and the night's shadows advanced.

"You look nice tonight, by the way."

Shock registered first at his words before a wave of anger took over. Seriously? Did he compliment her as he drove her who knows where against her will? "You do realize you kidnapped me, right?" His shoulders rose and fell in the dim confines of the car. "Michael, why are you doing this?"

"This never would have happened if you had gone out with me like I asked."

Disbelief reverberated down her spine. Now this was her fault? He hadn't seemed like he had a screw loose these last few months, but obviously her observation skills were lacking. She opened her mouth but closed it quickly. The words she wanted to spew would only make matters worse. Inhale. Exhale. "You kidnapped me because I wouldn't go on a date with you?"

"Oh no, my dear." A menacing chuckle

accompanied the sneer exposed by the dim lights from the dash. "This little adventure started years ago."

She frowned as confusion clouded her mind. "Care to explain?" Silence met her request. The ties binding her wrists pinched as she shifted.

"You don't remember me. Do you?"

What in the hell was he talking about? They had met before he took over Scott Enterprises' account? Her mind whirled as she tried to place him from her past.

"Don't remember? Not very flattering, Ms. Scott, but then the apple doesn't fall too far from the family tree. You Scotts have had it out for me and my family for quite some time."

His comments perplexed her. "You're going to have to spell it out to me what you are talking about."

"Isn't it ironic how I remember every little detail about you from the first moment I saw you."

She sensed his gaze upon her before his eyes focused back on the road.

"It was the summer after you graduated from high school. I attended the company's family picnic with my parents. You fascinated me with your tortoise shell glasses and smile full of braces."

The visual he painted made her cringe. She cleared her throat. "My grandfather used to have the best family picnics." Her mind raced as she tried to remember Michael as a young man. Shyness hampered her youth, and she had a hard time talking in new situations.

"You looked right through me then, but it was a different story when I appeared as an attorney. You didn't treat me as a kid from the wrong side of the tracks anymore."

A mental image of a gangly boy who offered to sit

with her at one of the picnics teased her mind. Further unease slid up her spine. This wasn't a spur of the moment kidnapping. "I'm sorry, Michael. I was so shy in my youth. If you tried to talk to me and I didn't reciprocate, it wasn't your fault." Her speech was met with more silence. The car fishtailed around another corner and Sierra slid slightly in the seat. He could have at least fastened her seat belt. Out of the side of her eye she took a tentative glance to the side mirror in hopes of seeing blue and white lights flashing behind them. More than disappointment fluttered in her stomach. No one followed. Had Riley found Cade to relay what had happened? "Michael. Why are you doing this?" A chill chased up her spine as an eerie laugh burst from his lips.

"My name isn't Michael."

****

Cade's boots crunched on loose rocks as he rushed behind the community building. He searched for clues as he surveyed the area. Deep grooves in the gravel indicated where Michael had sped away. He needed to get a look at the video cameras stationed in the vicinity.

"Sheriff. What's going on?"

The voice from behind him wasn't the one he wanted to hear at the moment. The question held an edge of steel. He turned and met Cora Scott's steady gaze. The teasing senior from less than an hour before was gone. This lady meant business and she deserved the blunt truth. "Ms. Scott. Sierra's been kidnapped."

A curse flew from her lips before her chin rose with quiet strength. "What's our move, Sheriff?"

Her calm intensity reflected in her gaze as it met his. "I need you to tell me what you know about the attorney working for Scott Enterprises."

"Michael Dunham?" Another curse erupted. "You think he's behind this?"

"I'm not sure until I examine the nearby camera footage, but Riley said Sierra mentioned the name Michael."

"I knew it." She pounded a fist against her hand. "I knew he was up to something from the moment we met."

Was Cora going to lose her cool? "You can kick yourself later. Right now, we need to gather my officers and make a plan of action."

She lifted her phone from her purse. "I'll call my friend at the FBI."

He placed a hand over hers to still her action. "No. Michael said no FBI. Until I talk to him myself. I need to know how stable he is."

She glanced down at her phone and frowned.

"What is it, Cora?"

"I've got a voicemail from Mark Simons. He's Sierra's Chief Financial Officer at Scott Enterprises." Her lips pursed together as she listened to the voicemail. "He wants me to call him right away. He'd been on the phone with Sierra when the call got disconnected."

"Put it on speaker."

Mark answered the phone on the first ring. "Cora. Thank goodness. I've been trying to get ahold of Sierra for the last couple of hours. She called me back, but we got disconnected."

"Mark, I have you on speaker phone. I have Sheriff Cade Collins with me." She swallowed hard before continuing. "Sierra's been kidnapped by Mr. Dunham."

"Damn it."

Cade leaned in. "Why did you need to get ahold of Sierra so desperately Mark?"

135

"I don't know if Sierra told you I was meeting one of the partners at Gates, Carey, and Bell this afternoon because Mr. Dunham missed his appointment with me yesterday morning. At three o'clock this afternoon I met with Mr. Gates. Inside the lobby there are pictures of the managing partners along with the other attorneys employed. Imagine my surprise when the picture of Mr. Dunham doesn't match the Mr. Dunham who has been serving as our counsel for the last two months."

"What?" Cora's shocked question registered above the music coming from the nearby building.

Cade held his frustration in check. "Can you explain?"

Mark cleared his throat, his own frustration apparent even over the phone's speaker. "The last two months have been a charade. I met the real Michael Dunham this afternoon. Once I asked Mr. Gates about the picture, we paid a little visit to Michael's house. Imagine Mr. Gates' surprise when he caught his wife there as well. In a very awkward situation."

Cade frowned as he tried to unravel what was going on. "Who's the man that's acted as your attorney over the last few months?"

"His name is Martin Driscoll. The gist of the story is Martin was blackmailing Michael because he was aware of the affair. A few months ago, the attorneys working with our account shifted and Martin concocted a way to pass himself off as the new attorney assigned."

"I understand he was blackmailing Michael, but what is the end game with passing himself off as your attorney?" The more Cade heard the more confused he became.

"Michael illuminated a little light on the situation. It

seems Martin's old man used to work for Scott Enterprises and was fired from his position."

Revenge. A groan made its way up his throat. One of the worst scenarios. "Was Michael able to shed any further information on Martin and where he may be taking Sierra? And why?"

"I don't believe he knew what Martin planned. He was just aware of the grudge against the Scott family."

The information wasn't much. But it was more than they had before the phone conversation began. "Thank you, Mark, for the details you've supplied."

"Sheriff. Let me know if I can help further." He paused and a deep sigh echoed over the speaker. "Please call me with any updates."

As the call disconnected Cade heard another low curse from Cora. "That no good ingrate."

He couldn't fault her language. "Cora. I need to check nearby security cameras." He turned to study her when she didn't answer. "Cora?"

She appeared lost in thought as she fingered the bracelet dangling from her wrist. "Was Sierra wearing a bracelet matching the one I'm wearing?"

He frowned as he tried to recall if she wore jewelry. "I believe so, but I'm not totally sure. Why?"

A smile broke across her face. "We've got the bastard." She slipped the piece of jewelry from her wrist and held it up for him to examine. "This has a built in GPS."

Delight traveled through him. "Is it active?"

A frown marred her brow. "No." She shook her head. "Sierra will need to activate it. I hope she remembers she is wearing it."

Chapter Twenty

The unnerving announcement echoed through her mind. His name wasn't Michael? She straightened in the seat as he made a left-hand turn. The asphalt turned to gravel and he slowed down. There weren't any yard lights or homes she could see. Where was he taking her? "What do you mean your name isn't Michael?"

He grunted but didn't answer her question.

"Where are you taking me?"

"I should have gagged you."

He glanced at her, but she couldn't read his expression in the dim interior. Questions weren't getting her anywhere. She tested the ties on her wrists again and heard the jingle of her bracelet. Hope burst in her chest. They hit a pothole and she banged her head against the passenger window. Now all she needed to do was survive the car ride. How far had they traveled from town?

The headlights illuminated a Sequoyah Bay State Park sign. He executed a turn and followed the sign into the park. There was a little bit of moonlight and she squinted at the passing signs. Had it read marina? Where was he taking her?

Less than a minute later they slowed and parked in front of a small cabin. "Home sweet home."

There was a dim yard light illuminating a drive covered with fallen leaves. A shiver traveled up her spine. Only one cabin had lights on. No one else seemed to be in the vicinity. He opened the car door and climbed out. As he crossed in front of the car he tripped and a curse carried in the still of the night. He opened her door and grabbed her arm to haul her out. She winced as she slipped and struggled to right herself.

The sound of keys jingling broke the quiet of the night right before an owl hooted a short distance away. He led her up a couple of steps to the door. The flashlight app on his phone lit up the key as he examined it.

"If you'd take these zip ties off, I could give you a hand."

He shined the light on the doorknob, inserted the key, and growled in her direction, "I've got it."

His hand left hers to search first her hips and then her chest.

"Hey." She screeched and shoved his hands away. "Keep your paws off."

He leaned in and turned the knob. "Just making sure you didn't have any weapons hidden anywhere."

She stumbled across the threshold and blinked at the bright light in the room. Claustrophobia had never been a problem. Until now. Her gaze landed on a queen size bed. The table and couch faded into oblivion in her mind. The fear she'd barely kept at bay until this point rose to the surface. She straightened her spine and turned to demand, "What do you plan on doing, Michael?"

He shrugged out of his jacket and placed it over the arm of the couch. "Your family owes me."

The tone of loathing in his voice threw her for a moment. Wherever the hate was coming from, it was deep seated. "Money?" She waved her bound hands to encompass the room. "Is this what all of this is about?" This whole scenario was premeditated, but for how long?

"Exactly." He clutched her upper arm and led her to the couch. "You see this little matter began years ago. Make yourself comfortable. Until I arrange for the money we're going to sit tight."

A sigh escaped. It was her turn to get annoyed. He was messing with her loved ones. "Help me understand something. Since we have time on our hands. Can you enlighten me on why you have a beef with my family."

A loud scoff passed his lips. "Your grandfather ruined my life!"

He'd indicated twice now her family destroyed his life. "How?"

"Shortly after the family picnic I last attended, your grandfather fired my dad."

She frowned and tried to wrap her head around his words. "Do you know why?"

"Sure. A trumped-up charge. Says my dad was embezzling. What a load of crap."

Was there some truth to the story and Michael had built up such bitter resentment he couldn't see the truth? Could she even reason with him? "What happened?"

He ran a hand through his disheveled hair. "What didn't happen? Dad started drinking heavily and we lost the house." Another glare was leveled in her direction. "For what? Because of a lie."

Her spine stiffened. "My grandfather wasn't a liar."

"And my dad was? Pfft." He sneered and said through gritted teeth, "Keep telling yourself that. Anything to make you feel better."

This argument wasn't going to prove anything. She inhaled a calming breath. Once again, she wondered how long he'd planned his revenge. Was the catalyst when her grandfather passed away? "Did you become an attorney with Gates, Carey, and Bell specifically to be counsel for Scott Enterprises?"

"Yes." A smirk tilted his lips. "It was orchestrated."

What did he mean? The more he talked the more perplexed she became.

With a jerk he started to pace across the room. "Why couldn't you have stayed on target with your normal routine?"

Trying to keep track of this conversation was becoming harder and harder. "You mean with my head buried in business?"

"Yeah." He threw his hands into the air. "Everything was going according to plan, until you took this impromptu vacation with Cora."

"And the plan was…?" She tried to splay her hands before she remembered they were fastened together.

His lips eased into a semblance of a smile. "Marriage, of course."

"What?" She jumped to her feet.

"But you didn't play by the rules, did you? You never even said yes to one date with me."

The pounding in her head intensified. "You're still not making sense."

"You're not the only one with plans." He turned and threaded his hands behind his back. "You have it all. Millions, a successful company, and a loving family. I'd hoped you would fall in love with me."

She raised her chin and scoffed. "Is it me or the millions you love?"

"One and the same." He shrugged his shoulders.

"No, it's not."

"Doesn't matter. You met the sheriff." His gaze met hers. "Yes. I know you like him and I'm pretty sure he's developed feelings for you. So, I decided to cut my losses. But before I do, I'm going to get a share of the pie."

She shifted and sat back down on the couch. "What makes you think they'll pay?"

"I have an ace up my sleeve. Your grandmother. She wouldn't take the chance of not paying the ransom."

He had a point. Blast it all. He recognized the fact. "Michael, would you be reasonable."

Laughter burst from his lips. "Have you not been paying attention? My name isn't Michael." He indicated the cabin. "Even if the sheriff searches, he won't find you before I get my money. The name Dunham isn't connected at all with this place."

"If you aren't Michael Dunham, then who are you?"

He rocked back and forth on his heels. "I guess it doesn't matter if you know the truth. I'll change my identity once I have the money."

A wave of relief flooded through her system. Maybe his end game wasn't to kill her.

"Martin Driscoll. At your service."

"Who is Michael Dunham?"

Her question interrupted his silent musings. "Michael sat beside me in my business law class in college. We became friends. And I used the friendship to my advantage." He sat down in a chair adjacent to her. "Michael made some poor choices, and I chose to capitalize on them."

Realization dawned. "You're blackmailing him? Aren't you?"

"I'd tried multiple times to pass the bar. I was visiting him one afternoon and he showed me an article about Charles Scott. His granddaughter was taking over the company now he had passed. Not long after, Michael was assigned as counsel for Scott Enterprises." He shrugged his shoulders. "I assumed his identity every time we had a meeting scheduled. You know the rest."

Stunned, she sat in silence at the elaborate scheme he described. What would have happened if he would have put more effort into passing the bar himself? She was having a hard time fathoming the web of deception he had spun. "How did you know I was in Harts Valley?"

"Easy. Twitter. Some ditz posted this morning you are in town, and she was planning on asking you to speak at some boring meeting."

Betsy. She was the reason he'd arrived in Harts Valley. "I think I'm going to be sick."

A snort escaped his lips. "But before you puke, it's time for you to make a call."

Chapter Twenty-One

Cade viewed the video footage from the hardware store closest to the fairgrounds. The blue sedan had headed south past the store. At least they had a little to go on. His cell rang. "What do you have for me, Travis?"

"The convenience store outside of town off of highway sixteen shows Michael's vehicle heading east."

Hmmm. Was he heading in the direction of the lake? There would be plenty of rentals available this time of year. An easy place to hide. "I'm heading back to check in with Cora to see if the bracelet app has been activated."

"I'm going to drive out a little farther. In case I can find any leads."

"Let me know if you make any discoveries."

Every light seemed to shine from Clara's home as Cade pulled into the drive. It didn't surprise him to see Riley run out to the porch as he exited his car.

"Dad. Did you find her?"

The look of hope faded from her features as he shook his head. Clara, Emily, and Cora had followed Riley out onto the porch. Emily wrapped her arms around his daughter's shoulders and escorted her back inside.

Clara turned but offered over her shoulder, "Come in, Sheriff. We have a pot of coffee going."

The porch steps creaked as he treaded up them. He

stopped and met Cora's gaze as she stood at the top.

"What do we know?"

"Surveillance cameras from the hardware and convenience stores show him traveling southeast."

Her brow furrowed into a frown. "Is that toward the lake?"

"Possibly."

An unladylike snort left her lips. "I've never trusted him." She stared off into the night and murmured, "For good reason it seems."

"Cora?" He waited until she focused on him. "How are you so calm right now? It's taking all of my years of training to stay levelheaded."

She threaded her arm through his. "Life with Charles wasn't easy. This isn't our first ransom, Sheriff."

They paused inside the threshold of the house. "What happened?"

"My daughter Felicia, Sierra's mom, fell in love her first year at college. Or what she believed to be love." She untangled her arm from his. "Everything turned out fine, but that fear never goes away." Her gaze met his. "Sheriff, it takes someone special to love a Scott. But I think you have what it takes."

Love? Was love the feeling bubbling under the surface of fear since he found out about the kidnapping? His thoughts scattered as the trill of a nearby cell broke into the silence.

Emily jumped up from where she sat. "That's Sierra's ring tone."

All eyes landed on the phone lying on the nearby end table.

Cora crossed over and picked it up. She held it out to him. "It's show time, Sheriff. You've got this."

He took a calming breath before answering. "Sheriff Collins."

"Good evening, Sheriff."

Irritation rose at the other man's cool assurance. "Dunham. Or should I say Driscoll?"

"Someone's been busy. Good to see you are on your toes, Sheriff."

A low growl crawled up his throat. "I want to talk to Sierra."

"I'm calling the shots." Anger tainted his calm. "I'll let Cora talk to Sierra. I know she's lurking about."

Cade held out the phone to Cora. "He wants you to talk to Sierra." Before she took the cell, he pressed the speaker button.

"I knew you were trouble, the moment I met you."

A deep chuckle reverberated over the speaker. "That's our feisty Cora. I've always liked your spunk. It's too bad my plan to become part of the family didn't work out like I planned."

She sputtered a moment. "As if."

"Someone here wants to say hello and then we will get down to brass tacks."

"Gram."

Cade's nerves calmed at the one firm word spoken from Sierra. Yes, the Scotts had moxie.

"Sorry this vacation isn't turning out like I'd planned." Cora leaned closer to him so he could hear the conversation clearly.

"Oh. That's okay, Gram. We'll be sipping rum drinks again on the beach in no time."

Cade watched as tension eased from Cora's shoulders. "I'm glad to hear it, my dear. Now put the blackguard back on the phone. Let's get this nasty business over so you can go back to canoodling with the sheriff."

"Sheriff? You there?"

He took the phone back from Cora. "I am."

"Here's the deal. I want three million by tomorrow noon."

His demand was ridiculous. His gaze locked with Cora's. "I'm not sure we can raise the money by noon."

"Sounds like a personal problem, doesn't it?"

Cade gritted his teeth and waited for the rest of the instructions.

"I want the money left near the Three Rivers Cemetery. Park in the back. There is a wooded area across from the back entrance. I've marked the stump with an orange flag."

"I don't know where the cemetery is."

"Google it." The words were bitten out through clenched teeth.

The line went dead, and Cade's gaze met Cora's. She still wore the aura of calm.

Her lips lifted into a smile. "Everything is going to be fine." Her gaze traveled to the other occupants in the room. "Please. Clara, Emily, and Riley, get some rest."

The room erupted with the surge of voices.

Cora silenced everyone with a wave of her hand. "Tomorrow is going to be hard enough. We all need to get some sleep. Please. Try to rest."

After a few more complaints from the other occupants in the room they shuffled off to bed.

Once again, he was amazed at her calm. "Can you get three million together before noon tomorrow?"

"I don't have to." She took a step away and eased down into the rocking chair.

N. Jade Gray

He frowned. Hadn't she participated in the same conversation he had moments before?

"Sierra will turn on the GPS when she can."

He frowned as he replayed the conversation in his mind. "How do you know?"

"She used our code phrase. Sipping rum drinks on the beach."

He'd thought it was an odd piece of information at the time but hadn't thought much more about it. "So, what is the plan?"

"We give her some time. I need to plug in my phone to make sure it's charged so we can track the signal." She indicated the sofa. "Have a seat, Sheriff." She rose and offered, "I'll get you the coffee I promised."

****

A calm settled over Sierra. She was going to be okay. "I need to use the restroom."

"It's through that door."

She held up her bound wrists. "It will be kind of hard with this on, don't you think?"

He pulled a pocketknife from his pocket and sliced the zip tie off. "It goes back on once you're done."

She nodded and rose. "Understood." The door clicked shut. There wasn't a window or any way of escape. She slipped off her bracelet. The specially made diamond bracelet winked at her in the dim lighting. She'd laughed at her grandmother when she'd presented it to her a couple of years ago. Who was laughing now? The button slid smoothly over to the on position. A sigh escaped as she attached it back onto her wrist.

"Hurry up."

The pounding on the door made her jump. "Hold your horses." She quickly used the restroom and washed her hands. A glance in the mirror above the sink showed the strain she'd been under this evening. The glint of her bracelet caught her attention. She ran a finger over the stones. Now all she needed to do was wait. Opening the door, Martin waited outside to confine her wrists once again.

"You'll sleep in there."

He indicated a room she hadn't noticed. There were two beds. A wave of relief swept through her body. "I'd like to lie down."

His eyes shifted into a squint.

"What?" She held up her hands. "I'm not Houdini. I'm tired." As she entered the room, she noticed a window. Was it big enough for her to get through if she was able?

"Don't even think about it." He leaned against the door jamb with his arms crossed. "I made sure it didn't open."

The scumbag had thought of everything. If only he would have put as much effort in making a living as he had this kidnapping, he'd be making bucks. She started to swing the door shut.

He stuck out his foot to stop it. "Leave it open."

The urge to slam the door in his face was strong, but she did as he asked.

"Don't try anything funny. I'm just outside your room." He turned and left.

A shiver made its way down her arms. The little room was nippy. Where had she left her jacket? She shook her head. It was back at the community building. As she crawled beneath the blanket, the cool sheets brought on another shiver. Now she was away from Michael, or rather Martin's knowing gaze, she let herself unravel. The strength she'd relied upon eked out of her very pores. A tear leaked out.

Gram and Cade were working on getting her out of this mess. Deep down she was aware of it in her heart. One thing this vacation had taught her was life is too precious to go around with your head stuck in work.

As her eyelids grew heavy, she envisioned a life with Cade and Riley.

Chapter Twenty-Two

It was barely five o'clock in the morning and Clara's home buzzed with activity. Cade and Cora started making plans as soon as the app indicated the GPS on Sierra's bracelet was activated. Emily, Clara, and Riley may have successfully slept for a couple of hours before coming back to join them in the living room. All three currently were tearing up newspapers to stuff into a ransom bag. Cora had decided not to give Martin a single red cent.

Draped across the dining room table was an area map Travis had brought from the station. Cade stood next to his deputy studying the map. His finger trailed over the area where the signal beckoned. "It looks like he's taken her somewhere within the Sequoyah Bay State Park."

Cora joined them and held up her phone. "I found the Three Rivers Cemetery." Her gaze focused on the piece of paper in front of them and trailed a finger over it until she tapped a spot. "It isn't far from the location of Sierra's GPS."

"Travis. I want you in the vicinity of the drop point." He examined the area. "We need eyes on both locations." His gaze met Cora's. "I'm guessing he won't have Sierra with him. While Travis has Driscoll in his sights, I'll sneak in and rescue Sierra."

Cora nibbled her lip and nodded. "I agree. He'll

leave her where he has her stashed."

"I'll take Deputy Stevens with me."

Cade nodded at Travis' suggestion. "Lay low and let me know when he's leaving the drop point. But don't arrest him. I want the honor."

"Yes, sir." Travis glanced over to where the ladies sat in the living room. "I'm going to check on how the ransom is coming along."

"Sounds like our plan is in motion, Sheriff." Cora's gaze met his. "I'd like to see the look on that no good rotten scoundrel's face when he realizes his payday isn't what he's expecting."

"Me too, Cora. Me too." She nibbled on her lip. One thing he hadn't witnessed from her since being introduced to her was nervousness. "Cora? Are you worried about the plan?"

She shifted and wrung her hands. "It's not that I don't trust your capabilities."

A feeling of foreboding climbed his spine. What had she done?

"Please, Sheriff. Promise me you won't get mad." Another nibble of her lip was executed before she blurted, "I called my friend, Will Sherman, who is an FBI agent and he's on his way." She grabbed his upper arm. "He is coming purely as an off the books favor."

Could he be frustrated with her maneuver? If he was being honest with himself, he was relieved to have someone with more experience to accompany him. What would Driscoll do if he caught wind an FBI agent was involved, actively or inactively? He shook his head. It didn't surprise him Cora had the direct number for an agent on her phone. "Cora. You're something else."

A sheepish look crossed her features. "So I've been

told."

He should reprimand her but couldn't find it in his heart to do so. "Thank you." He patted the hand still on his arm. "I appreciate the assistance."

"Sheriff. Why don't you rest for a bit? The shadows under your eyes aren't very becoming. The agent will be here soon. We'll wake you when he arrives."

Clara sidled up next to them. "Come on, Sheriff. I'm sure Sierra wouldn't mind if you rest on the bed she's been using."

The beautifully decorated bedroom didn't register as he sat on the bed. Exhaustion loomed in his mind and body. He scrubbed a hand down his face. What had started as an enjoyable day yesterday had turned into one of his worst fears.

Sierra's scent wafted to his nose as he laid his head upon the pillow. He inhaled deeply before sleep overtook him.

****

Sierra shifted as she tried to ease the crick in her neck. A dim light shined through the open doorway from the living room. Was Michael still awake? Or whatever his name was.

She leaned up on an elbow. A loud snore echoed from the other room. A cramp climbed up her arm at the awkward position. She eased back down on the mattress to relieve the discomfort. Tiny shadows danced across the ceiling as her gaze was drawn upward. What time was it? Had the signal worked on her bracelet?

Another loud snore came from the other room. Swinging her legs over the side of the bed, she rose and tiptoed to the doorway. Martin lay sprawled on the other bed with his back to her. She looked about for a clock.

Not spying one she carefully crossed the room and lifted a blind to glance out. As good as she could guess it was pre-dawn. The first fingers of light were beginning to glow in the sky.

A snort from her companion made her jump and jerk her gaze back toward the bed. He'd shifted and now lay on his back, but he was still sound asleep. She redirected her gaze back out the window. What the night had hidden the evening before was now illuminated. Scattered in the yard were trees spaced out with a scattering of brown leaves still hanging from the branches. Across from the cabin were boat slips in a cove of a lake. Isolated. There wasn't any hope of help coming from this area.

Which lake did she observe? They hadn't driven far from town. The sign she remembered from the night before had read Sequoyah Bay State Park. The lake most likely was Ft. Gibson. It wasn't an area she was familiar with. How had Martin had time to research the vicinity from the time he found out where she was until he'd abducted her?

She eyed the door with several chains and locks. There wasn't a way to leave without drawing attention to herself. Across the room was a small kitchen. Could she find something to saw through the ties binding her wrists? As quietly as she could she crept over to the drawers. Which one would hold the cooking utensils? She only had a limited amount of time to find what she was looking for. Sending a silent prayer skyward, she opened a drawer. It slid silently open. She cast a glance at the sleeping man before peering inside. The contents contained a small paring knife. Would it be sharp enough? The good news was the knife was small enough and concealed well as she slid it into her pocket.

Before he caught her snooping, she made her way back into the bedroom and sat down on the bed. She tested the zip ties on her wrists for probably the hundredth time. When the moment came for Martin to go collect the ransom money, she hoped he wouldn't tie her up. She needed time to saw through the plastic.

He appeared in the doorway of the bedroom giving her a start. Had he seen her take the knife?

"Do you need to use the facilities?"

She held out her bound wrists. "Yes." As she closed the bathroom door, she leaned against it and exhaled. He didn't know about the hidden blade. Knowing he wouldn't give her very long, she hurriedly took care of her personal needs. He stood where she left him when she opened the door.

"You hungry?"

Her stomach churned at the thought of food, but she needed to eat. Instead of answering she nodded.

"Sit down on that chair. I'll secure your hands while I'm gone."

With a stiff spine she crossed over to where he indicated and sat. She winced and leaned away from him as he tightened the ties and zipped them through an opening on the arm of the chair.

"I won't be gone long. I'm going to pop down to the Giggle Fish Grill."

He acted like there wasn't anything unusual about this situation. Making idle chit chat while he tied her to a chair. *Unbelievable*.

"Pancakes and sausage okay?"

"No." She tilted her chin. "I would rather have an omelet."

His shoulders rose and lowered. "I'll see what I can

do."

The sound of the key locking the door reverberated in the quiet of the cabin. A groan of frustration burst from her lips as she yanked her hands. Tears formed in her eyes and the waterworks irritated her more than she would like. She couldn't even wipe the evidence from her cheeks. She shrugged her shoulder and tried to wipe her wet cheek. Martin wasn't going to get the satisfaction of seeing her blubbering like an idiot.

Control. He wasn't going to win. The knife in her pocket was her secret weapon. When he left to collect the ransom, she would have her opportunity to escape.

A rooster crowing in the distance interrupted the silence. *Please. Please. Let her bracelet lead Cade and Gram to where Martin held her captive.*

Chapter Twenty-Three

Cade awoke with a start. A light tapping penetrated the sleep fog clouding his mind. He blinked as his brain registered how bright the room was compared to when he'd fallen asleep. Damn it, Cora had promised they'd wake him up. How much time had passed?

He wrenched the bedroom door open, and he headed down the hall. Every step he took inflamed his irritation. "Why didn't you wake me?" Everyone's chatter ceased as he entered the room.

"Sheriff. Meet FBI agent Will Sherman." Cora indicated an older man standing by the map on the table.

Cade ran a hand through his hair, glanced down, and silently counted to three. They hadn't meant any harm by letting him sleep. He hauled in a deep calming breath. "I'm sorry for my outburst." He took a step forward and offered a hand. "Nice to meet you. You've been briefed about the situation?"

"I have. And as Cora told you, I'm not on the clock. Don't worry about Mr. Driscoll finding out I am an FBI agent."

"Coffee, Sheriff?" Clara held out a steaming cup.

"I won't say no." His hand cradled the cup. "Thank you." The sip of the hot brew warmed him all the way down to his stomach. The map beckoned and he crossed over to stand by the table. "Will? Do you want to ride with me to the location we believe Sierra is being held?

Or do you want to go with Deputy Lakewood to make the drop and monitor the area?"

"Do you have backup going with you, Sheriff?"

Cade shook his head. "We are a small force."

"I'll ride with you then, Sheriff. If you don't mind."

His gaze met Will's. "I appreciate any assistance you can provide." The cell on his hip chimed. He answered and placed the call on speaker. "Travis. Did you find the drop off location?"

"Yes, sir. The bag was delivered. Stevens and I are a safe distance away in a stand of trees. We're going to hang out here until the allotted time."

Cade disconnected the call and glanced around at the other occupants of the room. It didn't surprise him Riley still remained. His gaze met his daughter's and she stood to make her way across the room.

"Dad. Be careful."

He smoothed back her hair and tucked it behind an ear. "I will."

She placed her arms around his waist and rested her cheek against his chest. "You'll let me know when Sierra is safe, won't you?"

He lifted her chin with a finger and met her gaze. "Absolutely."

"I love you, Dad."

He could feel the gazes of everyone in the room. "I love you too, kiddo."

****

The aroma coming from the bags Martin carried in would usually make her mouth water, but instead Sierra's stomach churned. He whistled an off-key tune, as if he didn't have a worry in the world. He placed the bags on the small table and turned with a smile. How she wanted to wipe the smug look off his face.

"Come get it while it's hot." A sarcastic chuckle rumbled from his chest. "Oh yeah. You can't."

The back molars hurt from where she clenched her teeth. It was going to take days to work out the tension in her neck from this ordeal. Was the anger surging through her body enough to overpower him if she got the chance? The only detail holding her back was the gun from the previous evening. She hadn't seen it since he held it against her ribs at the fairgrounds. If she made a move, would he produce it and shoot?

He produced the pocketknife from his pocket and cut the tie. "If you promise no funny business, I'll leave your wrists free so you can eat."

She bit back the snarky comment coming to mind and said through gritted teeth, "Much appreciated." No words were uttered as he unpacked the food. Could she cross to the door and escape quicker than he could react? Should she even chance it?

"Sit."

The single command made her jump. The glare he directed at her made up her mind. She needed to wait until he was out collecting the ransom. Settling in the chair she glanced at her companion.

"Planning your escape?"

She tore off a piece of paper towel and placed it in her lap before she opened the food container. "Yes. If you want to know the truth."

A bark of laughter left his lips. "Feistiness. Another Scott trait. You have that in common with your grandmother."

"I take that as a compliment."

His face turned serious. "Actually. I meant it as

one."

They ate in silence. Or more like he ate. She toyed with the food. The omelet was probably delicious, but her stomach remained in knots. With nervous fingers she waved the fork around to encompass the room, "How did you find our wonderful accommodations?" His gaze looked right through her for a moment. Did he choose to ignore her question?

"We had many family weekend trips to the lake when I was growing up." He shook his head and polished off his meal. "Until your family ruined mine."

Again, with the accusations. She took a bite and struggled to swallow.

He rose, gathered his trash, and dumped it in the nearby bin. "Are you finished?"

She glanced down at her meal. There were only a couple of bites taken. "I guess."

"It's almost time." He indicated the chair he'd previously secured her to. "Make yourself comfortable. I shouldn't be too long. That is if your grandmother and lover boy followed my directions."

****

Cade and Will sat a distance away behind a row of trees in an unmarked truck. Martin's car still sat in front of the cabin. He glanced at the clock on the dash. The time hadn't moved but a few minutes since the last time he looked. Nerves churned his stomach.

"Relax, Cade. We've got the upper hand."

Will had a point, but it still didn't make the waiting any easier. When the door to the cabin moments later opened, he straightened. They watched as Martin stopped outside the door and scanned the area. *Show time.*

Chapter Twenty-Four

Martin glanced back at the cabin and smiled. His plan was coming together. Sierra was tucked away. There was no way the sheriff or Cora could rescue her before he got the ransom money. His future was looking brighter.

Erring on the edge of caution, he gazed about. Nothing looked out of place to rouse his suspicion. His plan was foolproof. He'd retrieve the money and be on his way. All the hurt and anger toward the Scott family was about to be repaid. *This is for you, Dad.*

As he drove to the cemetery, he kept checking his rearview mirror. He'd stumbled across the Three Rivers Cemetery by accident when he was lost the previous day. Divine intervention. That's what it was. It's true he'd panicked a little when Sierra had disappeared for the week. All his well-laid plans were going up in smoke right before his eyes.

But everything changed when he'd seen the clueless tweet. He smiled and chuckled at his luck. A cheerful whistle burst from his lips. Today was going to be a good day.

He pulled into the drive at the back of the cemetery. There was a car parked at the front, but it didn't appear to be an unmarked police car. The owner of the vehicle appeared to be a young man who knelt by a headstone with a bunch of flowers grasped in his hands. He didn't put off a policeman vibe. Reassured the sheriff wasn't lying in wait, he pocketed his keys. The driver's door squeaked a little as he opened it and exited. That's one of the things he was going to buy with his money. A new car. A BMW. Or maybe a Mercedes.

Martin shook off his fancifulness and peered around before crossing the road to enter the deep brush. He'd marked a stump the day before with an orange flag he'd ripped off from a construction zone. The downed tree wasn't too far off the road, but remote enough to where someone wouldn't stumble across it. He glanced at his watch and quickened his pace. The drop was supposed to have occurred at noon. His payday should be delivered already.

The early morning dew had made the leaves wet, and they clung to his shoes. He shook one off in irritation. An exclamation of joy burst from his lips as he spied the camouflaged duffel bag resting near the stump. *Good ol' Cora had come through.*

He picked up the bag and placed it on the stump. The zipper stuck in his haste to open the case. It finally gave as he yanked harder. Disbelief filled his being as he stared down at the newspaper clippings stuffed inside. "No." The exclamation burst from his lips as he punched the case and it flew a few feet away. Something moved in the brush at the intrusion. Seconds later a skunk scurried away, but not before it lifted its tail and sprayed his stinky perfume all over him. His eyes stung and he cursed. Which made the situation worse. The acrid stench got into his mouth, and he gagged. After relieving his stomach of its contents, he straightened.

Still gagging he clenched his hands in fury. Pivoting he made his way back to the car. The Scotts were going to rue the day they messed with him and his family.

****

Sierra tilted her head. Had she waited long enough? Surely Martin had left. She eased the knife from her pocket. It irritated her that he'd zip tied both her right wrist and ankle to the chair. This was going to take longer than she expected. The blade was dull. A butter knife would cut better. After a few minutes of sawing, she stopped and flexed her left wrist. Was this a useless endeavor? She inhaled deeply before she continued trying to sever the plastic.

A gasp escaped as moments later the tie gave way and her wrist broke free. She bent and eagerly attacked the binding around her ankle. The sound of the doorknob rattling gave her pause. Panic flooded her mind as she frantically finished getting loose.

Her heart nearly pounded out of her chest as she ran across the room and stood behind the door. Surprise was on her side. Martin would expect to see her where he left her. She had the element of surprise on her side. If only she had a heavy object to smack him on the back of his head.

The door eased open in slow motion. She prepared to skirt around the edge and flee. A familiar scent reached her nose. *Cade*? Surely her weary brain was playing tricks. As if her mind had conjured him up, he eased into the room. A whimper escaped her lips and his gaze met hers.

"Am I dreaming?" Her legs began to tremble as she took one step.

In a few strides his arms wrapped around her in a tight embrace.

Words lodged in her throat as she pressed her cheek

against his chest and soaked up his warmth.

He eased back to cradle her face in his hands. His gaze scanned over her features before asking, "Are you okay?"

His voice was husky with emotion. She tried to shake her head. The tears pooled in her eyes leaked out down her cheeks. "I'm sorry." A sob lodged in her throat. "I'm so happy to see you."

"Ditto." He leaned in and captured her lips.

Warmth spread through her body. She looped her arms around his neck and moved in closer. A moan climbed her throat as the intensity of the kiss escalated. All the worry of the past few hours melted away. A throat clearing broke through her euphoria. Easing away from him she glanced over to see a gray-haired man standing inside the doorway.

"I hate to break up this hot tender moment"—the older man glanced out the open door—"but Martin is still out there."

Cade nodded and took a step back. "Sierra, this is Will Sherman."

Will tipped an imaginary hat in her direction. "Ma'am."

"Mr. Sherman." Knowing time was of the essence she asked, "What's the plan?"

Cade studied Sierra. He needed to get his head back on the capture of Martin. They'd wasted precious moments. Her stubborn tilt of her chin indicated she wasn't going to idly stand by while he did his job. "Sierra. I need you to go with Will. I want you to wait a short distance away." She began to argue, but he shook his head. "Listen. I need to focus on Martin's capture. I can't be distracted by whether or not you are safe." With his gaze he tried to implore her to listen. He breathed a sigh of relief as she nodded after a few moments.

"I'll go, but…" She caressed his face. "Be careful."

"Will, can you take Sierra to the truck? I'm going to find a place to hide and wait. I expect Martin back shortly. Stay close in case I need back up."

"I'll be right back." He took Sierra's elbow and led her from the cabin. "Your grandmother gave us a thermos with hot chocolate. It's waiting for you in the truck."

Cade waited until Will had Sierra safely a distance away before he studied the area. There was a clear line of sight of the porch from the neighboring cabin. He made his way around the back of the cabin and waited.

A flock of geese flew overhead. His gaze followed them until they gracefully glided down to land on the water. The waiting was always the hardest. Every time the occasional vehicle passed by his nerves would bunch in anticipation. In a nearby grouping of shrubs he spied Will as he inched forward to a grove of trees. He flashed him a thumbs up before he disappeared behind a massive tree trunk.

His cell vibrated in his pocket. Travis' message sent a wave of relief through him.

—Martin is on his way back. He's unarmed. We found his gun near the drop point.—

Tires crunching on rock drew Cade's attention. He peered around the corner and spied the dark blue sedan from earlier pulling up to the cabin. It was apparent from Martin's agitated gestures and the slamming of the car door he was angry. He wasn't going to be much happier once he found out Sierra wasn't in the cabin.

The other man continued to curse as he strode

toward the porch. An ominous odor reached Cade's nose. His eyes teared up from the potent smell of skunk. He pulled his pistol from its holster and made his way to the side of the cabin as Martin disappeared inside.

"Damn it."

The loud bellow scattered the geese in the cove across from the cabin. They took off in flight with a flutter of wings and loud honking. He stepped onto the porch. "Police. Get your hands up, Driscoll." The closer he got to the other man the more pungent the odor became.

Martin pivoted on his heel and glared. "I underestimated you, Sheriff. How did you find us?"

He shrugged off his question. "Does it matter?"

"Guess not." His shoulders lifted up and down.

Cade studied him. Hatred bounced off of him in waves. It was obvious he'd carried the animosity around for years. Was it wrong to antagonize him? He wrinkled his nose and sniffed the air. "New cologne. I can't say it's very flattering."

A growl started low in his throat before it emerged as a cry of outrage.

The attack came quickly. Cade was startled as Martin performed a karate kick and knocked the gun from his hand. He recovered quickly from the maneuver as he jumped forward and tackled him. They rolled a few feet as they wrestled to overpower each other. He elbowed him in the nose and took advantage of his howl of pain to recover his pistol a few feet away. "Enough." He tried to harness his ragged breathing. "Put your hands behind your back."

Blood trickled from Martin's nose and his hard stare challenged him.

"You heard the sheriff. Hands behind your back." Will stood inside the door's threshold with his own pistol leveled at Martin's chest.

Cade approached the man still on his knees. His handcuffs jingled as he placed them on his wrists. Martin continued to glower at him as he recited the Miranda rights. A few seconds later the cabin burst into a beehive of activity as Travis and Deputy Stevens rushed in to assist.

Martin's stare turned blank. "You know she'll tire of you. You don't stand any more of a chance than I did."

The scum had hit upon the one fear Cade had wrestled with since he found out Sierra's identity. A small hand cupped his arm and his gaze shifted down to meet a pair of beseeching hazel eyes.

"Don't believe the garbage he's spouting. I would love to give a relationship a try. Are you game?"

Several emotions were fighting to take control. Which one should he listen to? The heartache when Melissa passed crippled him for years. Was he brave enough to take on love again? Martin jerked his hands and jarred his arm. "Can we talk later? I need to process this arrest."

Chapter Twenty-Five

Disappointment flooded throughout Sierra's body. Was this the kiss of death for the relationship she'd hoped to have with Cade? "Sure." She took a step backward as his attention strayed away to police matters.

"Sierra?"

It took a moment for her name being called to permeate her brain. Not only was she exhausted from the ordeal, but disappointment washed over her as she wrestled with her hopes being dashed. Love seemed to be slipping from her hands. Her gaze met Travis'. "Sorry. I didn't hear what you said."

A look of sympathy settled in his eyes. "Don't let the sheriff's abrupt departure worry you. He does care for you." He placed a comforting hand upon her back. "Come on. Deputy Stevens and I will give you a ride back to my grandmother's house."

Numbness settled over her. The ordeal was over. Fatigue descended and all she could do was nod as he led her to his car. Travis and the other deputy tried to include her in small talk from the front seat, but she found it hard to participate. Overhead the sky was a gloomy gray and the passing scenery seemed just as dreary. All too soon they pulled into Clara's drive.

Tears leapt to her eyes as Gram, Emily, Clara, and Riley rushed out onto the porch. She had to wait for Travis to open the door but was soon gathered into a group hug a few steps away from the vehicle. All four tried to talk at once. "Hold on. One at a time."

"Is the scum locked up?" Gram's worried frown was firmly planted upon her face.

"Probably by now. Cade has taken Martin to the station." The tension eased from each of them at the news.

Riley hugged her once again and placed her head upon her shoulder. "I was so scared. I'm glad you're safe."

A lump materialized in her throat making it impossible for her to answer. She'd fallen not only for the sheriff, but for his adorable teenage daughter as well. Instead of answering she squeezed the teen harder.

Emily took a step back and didn't even bother hiding the fact she wiped tears away from her cheeks. "Riley wasn't the only one who was scared."

"I know." She met each gaze with her own briefly before continuing, "I love you all."

****

Cade closed the door to the cell. The resounding clang brought relief. He'd wanted to get Martin locked up as soon as possible. Away from Sierra. The outer lobby was eerily quiet as he made his way back to his office. Will waited inside lounging in one of his chairs.

"I know you're wanting to get back to Ms. Scott. I can stay and watch the prisoner." He pointed at the couch against the wall. "If you don't mind, I'm going to take a nap."

"Thank you, Will. For your offer and assistance today. It was comforting to know you had my back. Let me know if I can ever return the favor."

"I'll keep that in mind." He waved a hand. "Now.

Go. Check on your lady."

"One of my deputies should be back soon to relieve you."

Will tested a cushion before he lay down. "No hurry."

Cade fought the urge to put on the siren for a moment before he went ahead and flipped the lights on as he pulled away from the station. As he drove his thoughts wandered back to this afternoon and how he had left Sierra at the cabin. The hurt expression upon her face made him push down farther on the gas. He'd only wanted to get Martin away from her as soon as possible. But he was sure she'd misunderstood his rapid departure.

Travis and Deputy Stevens were getting ready to climb into their patrol car as he stopped abruptly in the yard.

"Sheriff? Everything okay?"

"Sorry." His gaze wandered toward the house a moment before he looked back at Travis. "I didn't mean to worry you by rushing in like I did. Will stayed at the station to watch over things. Are you heading back there now?"

"Yes. We'll check back in later."

He barely heard Travis' reply as he headed toward the porch steps.

"Where's the fire, Sheriff?"

Cora sat on the swing cradling a coffee mug. The twinkle that was absent only a few hours ago was back in her eyes. "I need to talk to Sierra."

"Well. Slow it down, cowboy. She's asleep." She patted the seat. "Care to join me?"

Did he have a choice? He swept his cowboy hat off and settled on the swing. "How is she?"

She squinted and watched him intently for a moment. "She's exhausted. Claims she needs a vacation from her vacation."

"Yeah. She didn't have much relaxation over the last twenty-four hours." Her direct stare was intimidating. "Is Riley still here?"

She shook her head. "Her Nanny picked her up a little bit ago." The coffee cup got placed on the nearby table. "Riley wanted me to relay a message to you though."

The executed wink threw him for a moment. "And what was the message?"

The swing rocked as she rose. "You'll have the house to yourself tonight. She's staying at Nanny's."

This woman relished in making him blush. He chuckled as he stood. "Noted."

Chapter Twenty-Six

Warm and comfortable, Sierra snuggled deeper into the mattress. As she squeezed her pillow a manly fragrance drifted to her nose. She smiled as she recognized Cade's scent. A deep longing had her blinking to wakefulness.

The room was no longer bathed in sunlight, but in shadows. How long had she slept? She stretched and tried to roll to her back. Except the motion was obstructed by a hard body. Fear erupted as she caught the slight fragrance of skunk and she tried to control the quiver shaking her frame. The nightmare wasn't over. She struggled to get out of the bed.

"Whoa. Relax, Sierra. It's me."

She twisted and focused on the man lying beside her. The beating of her heart didn't settle even though she recognized Cade. Wait. "How long have you been lying here?"

He rubbed a hand over his whiskered face before leaning up on an elbow. "A couple of hours. We both needed the rest."

"And you thought it would be okay to join me in bed?" She rose and took a few wobbly steps away. "After you abandoned me this afternoon without a backward glance?"

He was on his feet in seconds with his hands upon

her upper arms. "I'm sorry I left so abruptly." He dipped his head and tried to catch her gaze. "Leaving was the last thing I wanted to do this afternoon. But I had to get Martin away from you."

She finally met his beseeching gaze. "Why?"

As his hands fell away from her arms, so did the warmth. He turned and paced a few feet away. "It took all of my professional training not to beat him for what he'd put you through."

Had she misinterpreted his desire not to talk this afternoon? She nibbled on her lip. "Cade?" She waited until he turned and met her gaze. "I'm only going to ask this once more." A quick inhale and exhale gave her the courage she needed to ask, "Do you want to give a relationship a try?"

An uneasy expression crossed his features. "I'm just a country sheriff."

He hadn't said no. Hope surged. "That's not what I asked, Cade."

"We are so different."

Was he arguing with her or himself? It seemed she wasn't the only one who felt confused. She took a step toward him. "Again. Not what I asked."

"Damn." He met her in the middle of the room. "You've been on my mind almost every waking moment since I met you."

"Finally, we're getting somewhere." She took the final step into his arms and leaned against his chest. "You don't think I'm not scared?" She glanced up to look into his downcast gaze. "It's not only you and me in the equation."

"Riley?" A crooked smile twitched at his lips. "Trust me, she's on board." He wiggled his eyebrows up and down. "She left a message for me. She won't be home tonight. In case you are interested."

Now it was her turn for her heart rate to speed up not from fear, but with anticipation. Rising on her tiptoes she grazed his lips. "Sheriff. As much as I love you in uniform, I can't wait to see you out of it." She chuckled as his Adam's apple bobbed and his gaze slid to the door. "I do believe we'd be more comfortable at your place." She trailed her fingers over his chest. "Don't you agree?"

He gave her a swift kiss and grabbed her hand. They crossed the room to stop by the window. He dropped her hand only to slide it open. A chilly breeze flowed through the opening and made the curtains flutter.

She quirked a brow and a nervous giggle escaped. Did he expect her to climb through?

"Ladies first." He gestured with a hand for her to crawl out.

Shock rippled down her spine. He really did expect her to climb through the opening. "What are we doing?"

He placed a finger to his lips and whispered, "Avoiding the Spanish inquisition."

As he said the words it dawned on her what he meant. There was no way Gram and Emily would let her disappear for the evening, especially after the ordeal from the night before. "Okay. But I need to at least leave a note. I for one don't want our evening interrupted." A giddy excitement made her hands shake as she searched for something to write on. She finally pulled a receipt from her purse. Flipping it over, she paused. *What was she going to tell them? Don't you dare call me if you know what's good for you? And don't call Cade either?* With a chuckle she wrote quickly.

Cade looked over her shoulder to see the words. A

soft chuckle rumbled in his chest. "Ready?"

She glanced down at the ratty sweatshirt and lounge pants she wore. Should she change? A glance into his eyes proved what she wore didn't matter. "Good to go."

Chapter Twenty-Seven

Cade sat behind the wheel and shook his head. He'd climbed out of a window like a randy teenager. They had made it to the vehicle without being detected, but he hadn't started the engine. If Riley ever found out what he'd done…his parenting skills would be questioned.

"Cade? Is everything all right?" Her hand snaked across the console and touched his arm. "You haven't changed your mind, have you?"

It dawned on him he had, but not in the way she meant. He didn't need time to consider a relationship with her. What would Sierra say or do if instead of sneaking off for a passionate lovemaking session he asked her to marry him instead? Tonight? Once the idea formed in his mind, he couldn't shake the feeling that was what needed to happen. She sat waiting with an eyebrow quirked. His gaze sought hers in the dim lighting cast by a nearby yard light and locked his fingers with hers. "I was over here berating myself for the example I'm setting for my teenage daughter."

The disappointment was apparent as her fingers tensed within his and her shoulders lowered in resignation. "I understand."

No. He didn't think she understood at all. He brought their entwined hands to his lips and kissed the back of her hand. "Sierra. I know we haven't known each other long. But I've always been a man to go after what

I want. And I want you. Not for just this evening." He kissed her hand again. "But forever."

A gasp escaped between her lips. "Are you asking me what I think you're asking?"

"Yes." He nodded and leaned in closer. "Will you marry me?"

"Ah." The element of surprise left her speechless for a moment. Her gaze left his to glance at the house. "How does this alter our evening's outcome?"

"Oh. I still plan on making love to you." He let go of her hand and reached into his coat pocket for his phone. "I have Judge Murphy's number. He owes me a favor."

She chuckled and shook her head. "Does everyone in this town owe you?"

Smiling he said, "Pretty much." Once again, he grasped her hand. "In all seriousness. I'm asking you to marry me. Now. Tonight." Her disbelief and hesitation gave him pause. Had he read the situation wrong? Was this nothing more than a vacation fling for her after all?

"Gram will be pissed."

His heart stuttered in response to the twinkle of merriment sparkling in her eyes. Did this mean she'd marry him? "I know what I'm proposing is crazy, but this feeling I have for you…" The words he wanted to say got stuck. "I love you."

A determined glint entered her eyes and her chin rose a notch. "It's me you love, right? Not a million other reasons why you think you do?"

Of course, she was talking about her wealth. The money hadn't even entered his mind. "That's something else we can have the judge draw up tonight if it would make you feel more comfortable. I'm not after your money." He wiggled his eyebrows. "Now your body is another story."

"You'd do that for me?"

The words were whispered, but he heard them clearly. "Want to seal it with a kiss?"

"Absolutely." She closed the distance between them and placed a tender kiss upon his lips. "Make the call."

The murmured words staggered him. "Is that a yes?" At the answering nod he dialed.

****

Sierra should have changed her clothes. She stood in front of Judge Murphy and his wife in her ratty sweats and sweatshirt. Cade held her hand and gazed into her eyes as he repeated the vows the Judge spoke. The last twenty-four hours were so surreal. Would she wake up to find that it was a dream?

"Sierra?"

She jerked to attention to find all eyes upon her. A wave of heat flooded her cheeks as she realized she'd missed the prompt to murmur her vows. After she cleared her throat, she repeated the words that united them in marriage.

"By the powers vested in me for the State of Oklahoma, I now pronounce you husband and wife." He paused and winked at Cade. "You may kiss the bride."

A happy gleam lit Cade's eyes as he leaned down and captured her lips in a gentle, but passionate kiss.

The drive from the judge's house to Cade's was made in comfortable silence. Sierra's hand tingled where he softly caressed it with his thumb. From the corner of her eye, she studied him by the truck's dash lights. *This is crazy.* She bit her lower lip and sat up straighter when they parked in front of his home. What she could see in the moonlight was a ranch style house. Possibly brick.

"Welcome to our home. Hold tight and I'll get your door."

As he crossed in front of the truck in the moonlight, she was reminded of the evening they first met. She smiled as he opened the door. A squeal erupted from her lips as he swung her up into his arms.

"I'd be neglecting my groom duties if I didn't carry you across the threshold."

The muscles bunched in his arms, and she snuggled in close. A feeling of being home overtook her. All too soon he lowered her to the floor across the threshold of his house. He flipped the hall light on, and she took a few steps into the room. The living room was homey, warm, and inviting. A bookcase surrounded the fireplace, and the shelves were full of books and knickknacks.

His arms wrapped around her waist from behind and he nibbled her neck. "Are you hungry?"

She tipped her head so he could have better access. A sigh escaped as she asked, "For food? Or for love?"

"Either." His breath skittered across the skin he'd exposed on her shoulder.

Turning in his arms, she captured his lips with her own. Warmth traveled down her spine as he took the opportunity to explore her back, waist, and hips with his hands. She broke the kiss. "Is your bedroom on this excursion? Or am I expected to do a self-guided tour?"

"Mmm." He laced his fingers with hers and led her down a nearby hallway.

She barely noticed the family photos lining the walls. Fingers of light illuminated the wood floors at the end of the hall. She paused before crossing into his bedroom. A small lamp sat on a small table in the corner of the room. But that wasn't what caused her to pause. "Um." Clearing the huskiness from her throat she tried again, "Texas, we have a problem."

His gaze bounced from hers to the bed. A frown furrowed his brow. "I made the bed. What's the problem?"

She stared at the bedspread and shook her head. "There is a huge hitch already in our wedded bliss. We didn't finish our discussion on which Oklahoma College you support."

His gaze shifted to the University of Oklahoma bedspread. A brow inched upward in question. "Are you saying this is a game changer?"

Shock was apparent in his voice and she tried to contain the giggle that threatened. "This room will be redecorated. Or we will be getting an annulment or divorce."

A stammered laugh emerged from his lips. "Are you serious?"

"As a heart attack." She crossed her arms across her chest.

A determined glint eased into his eyes. He closed the gap between them. "I knew this marriage wasn't going to be easy, but I'm willing to have our first fight so we can make up."

The laughter she'd held back gurgled from her lips. "Your face. Priceless."

His gaze was as tender as a caress as he reached up and began to unbutton his uniform.

The merriment dried up as he eased out of his shirt and exposed his chest. Her knees weakened as he closed the remaining gap between them, and his mouth descended. Passion unfurled in her belly. Gone were the tentative kisses. Heat permeated from his bare chest. Her sweatshirt rose as his hands moved underneath. His stroking fingers sent pleasant shocks through her. Cool air hit her heated skin and she gasped.

He dropped her sweatshirt to the floor and broke off the kiss. His voice was a husky rasp as he whispered, "You're stunning."

Sierra had never felt more beautiful than in this moment. His gaze held a warmth and wonder she'd never experienced before. Her gaze locked with his as she unclasped her bra. His breath hitched as the lacy undergarment joined her shirt on the floor.

The pad of his thumb brushed intimately one breast and then the other.

Her nipples firmed at the caress. She arched into his touch. A tremor skittered down her back as her breasts grazed his chest. She savored the feeling a moment before she leaned in to place her lips on his hardened nipple.

A low groan hissed from his lips. "Sierra. I'm trying to go slow here."

She smiled and nibbled again. "Slow is for pansies." An excited shriek echoed in the room as he tossed her gently onto the bed.

He leaned over with a knee beside her on the bed to nuzzle her taut nipples, rousing an ache deep inside. Her knees trembled when his lips slid across her belly and his hands slid her sweatpants from her body.

Desire had her hands trembling as she reached to unbuckle his belt. She felt him shiver at her touch. He rose and discarded his pants. A gasp escaped as he lowered his hard body atop hers. She squirmed as she tried to get closer. His gaze connected with hers as she welcomed him into her body. The waves of pleasure throbbed through her as they found harmony in their movements. Soon their bodies vibrated with a shuddering ecstasy.

Heart pounding, she closed her eyes. Lord almighty. His uneven breathing beside her gave her satisfaction. She twisted her head to study him. He had an arm flung over his eyes as he tried to calm his breathing. Joy rose inside her. "There will be no living with Gram now, you know."

He peered at her from under his arm. "I owe Cora a debt of gratitude."

"Oh. Please." She moved over to settle her body against his chest. "Don't build her up any more than she is already."

His arms wrapped around her. "I'll build her up as much as I like. Would we have met if she wouldn't have pulled the disappearing clothes act?"

"Absolutely." She planted a kiss on his lips. "We would have found a way."

"I love you, Mrs. Collins."

"I love you too, Sheriff." She glanced about his bedroom. "Now. Let's discuss your bedroom decorations and how they need revamped."

A word about the author…

N. Jade Gray grew up on a farm in Oklahoma with one sister and three brothers.

She began reading romance novels in high school and was hooked. In an attempt to entertain her friends, she began writing stories. The biggest hurdle she had to overcome was sharing her stories. She's been a member of the following writing groups, the Wichita and Regional Authors, Low Country Romance Writers, and Romance Writers of America. She currently is a member of the Ozark Romance Authors group.

She met her husband while attending college and has two grown sons. Her oldest son is married and has two daughters.

Not really knowing what she wanted to do when she grew up, she's held various jobs in the accounting and legal fields. She lives in Missouri with her husband, rescue cats Meera, Mango, and Pancake, and one spoiled dog-named Fabio. Yes, she helped name the dog. She loves to hear her husband calling for his four-legged companion.

www.njadegray.com

Thank you for purchasing
this publication of The Wild Rose Press, Inc.

For questions or more information
contact us at
info@thewildrosepress.com.

The Wild Rose Press, Inc.
www.thewildrosepress.com

Milton Keynes UK
Ingram Content Group UK Ltd.
UKHW020730081123
432193UK00018B/625